KU-636-863

JILL BARRY

HOME TO MISTY MOUNTAIN

HIGHLAND
LIBRARIES

Complete and Unabridged

(90015598)

LINFORD
Leicester

First published in Great Britain in 2018

First Linford Edition
published 2020

Copyright © 2018 by Jill Barry
All rights reserved

A catalogue record for this book is available
from the British Library.

ISBN 978–1–4448–4357–6

Published by
F. A. Thorpe (Publishing)
Anstey, Leicestershire

Set by Words & Graphics Ltd.
Anstey, Leicestershire
Printed and bound in Great Britain by
T. J. International Ltd., Padstow, Cornwall

This book is printed on acid-free paper

HOME TO MISTY MOUNTAIN

UK-born Hayley Collins is visiting Australia, staying with a friend and looking for work. Craig Maxwell runs a holiday resort at Misty Mountain, a four-hour drive from Melbourne. When Hayley applies to be an administrator at the resort, Craig takes her on — and much else besides. She has to return to England in twelve months. He's engaged to a woman whose father is helping to keep the resort's finances in the black. So when Hayley and Craig fall in love, it seems a future together is only a distant dream . . .

Books by Jill Barry
in the Linford Romance Library:

DREAMS OF YESTERDAY
GIRL WITH A GOLD WING
THE SECRET OF THE
SILVER LOCKET
A CHRISTMAS ENGAGEMENT
MRS ROBINSON
CHRISTMAS REVELATIONS
CHRISTMAS IN MELTDOWN
PUPPY LOVE
SUMMER LOVE
MALLORCAN MAGIC
LOVE ON TRACK
LOVE STRIKES TWICE

Where the Heart Is

'Oh, no! Please don't do this to . . . '

Hayley's words melted into the Melbourne night as the balcony door slammed.

She had wandered outside for a breath of fresh air before bed, but these October nights could turn nippy, especially when you were wearing nothing but a nightshirt.

The courtyard below was deserted. Her phone was inside the apartment. And her friend Jacqui was attending a work function, leaving Hayley facing a teeth-chattering couple of hours.

She daren't risk leaning too far round the trellis separating the adjoining balcony. But Jacqui had said her neighbour was in residence, so should she yell for help? She groaned aloud.

'Hello? Are you all right out there?'

'Oh, thank goodness! I locked myself

1

out and my friend's not due back for ages.'

'Is that an English accent?'

What difference did that make when she so obviously needed rescuing?

'Top marks!'

Her neighbour peered round the trellis, allowing her a glimpse of dark hair, brown eyes and stern expression.

'Sorry if I sounded rude,' she apologised quickly. 'I've only been in Melbourne about five minutes.'

'And already you're in a pickle?'

Hayley heard him walk away.

'Hello?' Surely he hadn't abandoned her to the Australian night? She closed her eyes again, trying not to panic. Surely the sarcastic man with the gorgeous voice would be back?

She breathed out as he spoke again.

'Here, grab this before you get hypothermia.' Hayley reached for the fluffy white robe. 'It belongs to my fiancée but your need's greater than hers just now. My name's Craig Maxwell and I'm about to contact the night manager.'

'Thank you, Mr Maxwell. I'm Hayley Collins.'

'He'll need permission from the tenant. You don't look like a cat burglar, so that'll be your friend, I guess?'

A cat burglar? Hayley gulped.

'Yes. I hope the office has Jacqui's mobile number because . . . '

'You can't access it right now.'

'Precisely,' she said wearily.

'No worries. You'll be back inside before you know it.'

Hayley relaxed a little. Maybe she'd misjudged Craig Maxwell. He didn't need to be nice to her, but it certainly helped.

★　★　★

'Did you find out anything about him?' Jacqui poured black coffee into pink polka-dot porcelain mugs.

'Our discussion wasn't exactly cocktail-party chit-chat.' Hayley buttered a slice of toast.

'It's lucky you were rescued before

3

the temperature plummeted. Did Mr Maxwell hear you shout for help or was he already on his balcony?'

'I hadn't begun yelling. Craig must've wandered outside and heard me muttering.'

'So it's Craig, is it? I'm surprised he didn't wait until I got back. Men like being seen as brave and protective.'

'I don't think phoning the night manager can compare with dragon slaying!' Hayley giggled. 'And, Craig Maxwell has a fiancée, which reminds me, I need to have her robe laundered.'

'When he first moved in, there was a blonde woman around but I don't think she lives here.'

'I'm not surprised he's spoken for — he's definitely eye candy.' Hayley pictured her rescuer's chiselled cheekbones, glossy hair, the curls tamed but still nestling upon the nape of his neck. But, more importantly, something in his eyes had intrigued her.

'He's attractive, but I prefer a warmer, friendlier type, like Cameron,'

Jacqui said. 'He's a teddy bear! To be fair, whenever our paths cross, your knight in shining armour always speaks, but I still find him kind of daunting.'

'As he's seen me in my nightshirt, I'd say the ice has been cracked if not broken.' Hayley spotted her friend's smirk. 'Come on, he's engaged to be married!'

'Are you disappointed?'

'I don't have time for dating.' Hayley knew her friend was tactfully avoiding mentioning Dan. All that was still too raw to discuss. 'My priority is to find a job and somewhere to live. Your boyfriend Cameron won't want me hanging around once he's back.'

'You're welcome to stay as long as you want.' Jacqui drained her cup. 'Shall we get ready to go out now? We'll take a tram to the city and I'll show you some of my favourite stores and cafés.'

'Brilliant. I'll tackle the agencies on Monday.'

'Don't forget the employment websites. At least we're into the main tourist season now.'

'I'm used to working in an office but, if it comes to it, I'll happily put on a pinny.'

★ ★ ★

Next door, Craig Maxwell reached for his glass of iced water. After a weekend escorting his demanding fiancée Leila to parties, Monday morning brought a mix of relief and apprehension.

Relief because he could abandon his social face and apprehension as to whether he'd find someone prepared to tackle an unusual job.

At his family's country resort, the position of receptionist/administrator — more like Jill or Jack of all trades — still remained vacant.

Exactly as he'd wanted to do after college, most of the bright young folk raised in the area couldn't wait to start their gap year or head for the city to fulfil their dreams among Melbourne's teeming districts.

Craig couldn't afford to pay a big wage and, with strong competition within the holiday industry, he badly needed a bumper season. He daren't confide this to his parents, being determined they should enjoy their twilight years.

The woman engaged for maternity leave cover had backed out, leaving him at square one. He'd need to contact the agency and hope someone was prepared to trek from the city out to prime kangaroo territory.

The area didn't suit everyone — his fiancée included — though Craig loved the place and, given his way, would live there permanently.

But Leila felt differently, though neither of them seemed prepared to face that situation, something bothering Craig more and more. It wasn't only that she assumed he'd back down, it was the way she couldn't understand his commitment towards Misty Mountain.

Leila wanted her fiancé with her in

7

the city. His heart was in the country.

Craig got to his feet, intent on contacting the agency. He had a ruby wedding anniversary party looming, plus several spring bridal parties booked.

His staff were already overworked and he knew most of them stayed through loyalty or because their families lived locally.

This dedication helped create the friendly atmosphere his family strived to achieve and Craig didn't intend to destroy it. Nor did he relish sucking up to his future father-in-law, but if that was what it took . . .

★　★　★

'Where's Misty Mountain?' Hayley looked up from her laptop.

Jacqui put down her magazine.

'What makes you ask?'

'They're advertising an interesting job vacancy.'

'I think Cameron's mum and dad

once spent a long weekend there. If that's the same place, it's a four-hour drive from the city. You wouldn't want to go all that way for an interview and find the boss looked a bit dodgy, now would you?'

'True, but luckily they're interviewing in the city the day after tomorrow.'

'Will you apply?'

'I'm certainly thinking about it.'

Jacqui peered at the laptop screen.

'So, not a permanent position?'

'No, but my visa only allows me to stay up to twelve months.'

'Aw, Hayley, I'm enjoying having you around again.'

The two girls had worked for the same company in London until Jacqui's parents decided to emigrate and she opted to accompany them. Cameron was one of her first clients when she began working for a Melbourne car rental firm.

Hayley looked up.

'You have a boyfriend and I wouldn't want to intrude. I'll need to move out soon, even though I love being here. It makes sense to apply for this job and if nothing comes of it, I'll look for something else and find a flat share.'

Jacqui shrugged.

'You seem to have it all sorted. I hoped you'd be around longer than a few days, though.'

'I haven't gone yet. Let me check their website.' Moments later she leaned back in her chair. 'How about that?'

'Wow! Fantastic scenery, but that probably means snakes and spiders! It'll be a bit different from taking the Tube to work on a dismal London Monday.'

'Hang on, did you spot this?' Hayley was reading the 'About Us' page. 'That name seems familiar. Coincidence? Or could it be the man next door?'

Jacqui examined the wording.

'Hmm . . . I've no idea how common that surname is here. If the Craig Maxwell you met is the one offering that job and you apply, at least he's already met you.'

'I wasn't dressed to impress, remember.'

'No, and obviously, I'd prefer you to find a job locally, but maybe Fate's trying to tell you something?'

Hayley smiled.

'I'll apply and see what happens.'

Craig Maxwell may have saved her from a shivery couple of hours but she hoped the man she'd met wasn't the one advertising this job. She began filling in the online application: At least she'd made a start on job hunting.

A Breath of Fresh Air

Next morning, Hayley travelled to the city centre. She'd dressed to look smart and wore a crisp white shirt, pale grey trouser suit and heels.

With time to spare, she strolled into a shopping arcade, telling herself not to explore too far. At precisely five minutes to ten, she walked back on to the main street and pushed open the agency's door.

A woman, neat in navy blue, glanced up from her computer.

'How may I help?'

'I'm here to see Mr Maxwell. My name's Hayley Collins.'

The receptionist's eyes widened.

'You're British, right?'

'I have the relevant travel and work visa.'

'No worries.' The woman smiled. 'Your accent makes a nice change.' She

12

checked something on her computer. 'Take a seat, Hayley. I'll let Mr Maxwell know you're here.'

'Thank you.' She sank on to a black leather couch and sat, knees together, handbag perched on her lap, wondering what she'd let herself in for.

Soon, the receptionist called her name.

'Take the elevator to the third floor and Mr Maxwell will meet you.'

Hayley leaped to her feet, dropped her handbag and wished she'd done one of those courses where they taught you to be ladylike. Sometimes she hated her long legs and larger than average feet though Jacqui, a good five inches shorter, insisted she envied her friend's model girl appearance. This helped her feel more confident as she pressed the call button.

At the third floor, she stepped outside and spotted a door marked Conference Room which opened to reveal a tall figure.

'We should stop meeting like this.' Craig Maxwell leaned on the door-frame, arms folded across his broad chest.

Last time she saw him, he'd worn a faded crimson T-shirt and dark jeans but today he looked the perfect city businessman. Somehow she found the words to greet him.

'Come in, Hayley,' he continued. 'May I offer you a coffee?'

Who'd have thought he could be so friendly?

'Only if you're having one, Mr Maxwell.'

'That's a yes, then.' He walked over to a table where coffee paraphernalia waited. 'Please have a seat. May I ask if you knew who I was when we met the other night?'

Did he think she expected favourit-ism?

'Definitely not. I hadn't even begun job-hunting.'

'Right.'

Hayley's tummy lurched.

14

'You told me your name, of course, but when I checked your website, I'd no idea whether you were Jacqui's neighbour or not.'

'That's understandable. For all I know, there might be several Craig Maxwells.' He poured coffee. 'Help yourself to milk and sugar. I should tell you I've seen two other candidates with another two due later.'

She nodded.

'No ill effects from your balcony exploits, I hope?' He caught her eye and grinned.

'None, thanks. Your fiancée's robe has been laundered, by the way. I wasn't sure whether to leave it with the concierge.'

'That'll do fine.'

He was examining a print-out of her CV.

'You're over-qualified for this position. You do realise that?'

She lifted her chin.

'Yes, but Mr Maxwell . . . '

'Please,' he interrupted, 'I prefer

Craig. Tell me why you want to leave the city.'

'I need to find employment. Jacqui's fiancé returns from his trip next week and I don't want to be in their way though she insists I can still stay.

'I love what I've seen of Melbourne but the position you're offering is the perfect solution. It sounds interesting as well as offering accommodation.'

He raised his eyebrows.

'Interesting being the operative word. You do realise this is maternity cover?'

'That's one of the reasons it attracts me. My visa doesn't allow me to stay here after next November.'

'I notice you've had control of your own staff. How will you react to becoming the junior member of the team? Your duties would include much more than admin and dealing with guests.

'I'm not saying you'd be expected to cook breakfasts but you could find yourself collecting guests from the station or advising them what to do if they come face to face with a snake.'

He was challenging her. She ignored her panic at the thought of snake charming and smiled.

'I'm a stranger in your country and I'll welcome my colleagues' instructions and advice. Particularly regarding snakes.'

'Touché! I'm not trying to frighten you — far from it.'

'Believe me, I don't have a problem with accepting orders and I think you'll find I'm polite and calm under pressure.'

To her relief, he nodded.

'You certainly proved your ability to keep your cool the other night.' He steepled his fingers beneath his chin. 'So, what special qualities could you bring to my business?'

Her mind went blank.

'Erm, I enjoy talking to people.'

'Good. And those holiday hotel jobs?'

'I took those in my uni vacations so I didn't keep sponging from my parents.'

Was that an approving look?

'I soon learned how a pleasant smile

and friendly greeting helps put you on a good footing, and I like the old-fashioned idea that the customer is always right.' She hesitated. 'I enjoy helping keep a successful organisation running that way.'

'That attitude's certainly in keeping with our beliefs, Hayley. Also, your ability to drive will be useful. Most of our guests arrive by car but we ferry them back from the restaurant if they're not comfortable driving after dark.'

She forced a nod. Luckily, he was looking at his notes. I'll deal with that problem when I'm forced to, she told herself.

'We like our visitors to sample wines from our cellar, so a lift back to their guest cottage is a very important part of the package.'

'Of course.'

He hesitated.

'I take it you're not allergic to marriage? Weddings are a speciality of ours.'

She recalled Dan's face when he had

announced they were finished.

'I've attended weddings of family and friends, so I can't imagine being jealous of the bride and spiking her drink, if that's what you mean?'

Was her response too cheeky? But Craig Maxwell was laughing.

'You really are a breath of fresh air, Hayley! Can you get up early, for a six o'clock shift?'

'No problem.'

'How about split shifts?'

'You mean like eight till one then six till late? I'm good at snatching a few hours' sleep and bouncing back.'

'You're certainly in good shape.' Hastily, he consulted his paperwork. 'I mean, you look very healthy. There's a fair bit of running round but we insist upon adequate rest breaks and leisure time for our staff, even an occasional day off.'

He met her gaze.

'You know the going rate. You'll be well fed and our staff cottages, though I say it myself, are more comfortable than you'd find in many other resorts.'

She nodded.

'If I were to offer this position, could you travel to Misty Mountain a couple of days from now?'

'I don't see why not.'

'Excellent.' She watched him write something down.

'I'd need to look up trains, I imagine, if I got the job?'

'Don't worry about transport. I need to check on your availability because time is of the essence.'

'I understand.'

'Right, then, I'll be in touch later today, one way or the other.' He glanced at her CV again. 'I have your mobile number plus your friend's.' He rose.

She stood and held out her hand, enjoying having to look up at him.

'Thank you so much for seeing me, Mr — erm, Craig.'

He shook her hand.

'I'll walk you to the lift. Know your way home? Got the tram number?' That disarming grin again.

'I do, thanks. Jacqui's briefed me.'

He waited with her after pressing the elevator call button.

'I forgot to say, you can claim travel expenses if you ask the receptionist for an application form.'

She shook her head.

'I wanted to come into the city so I shan't take up your kind offer. I might drop into another agency or two — just in case.'

'Fair enough. I like your style. Have a good day and I promise we'll speak soon.'

Hayley was conscious of his gaze upon her as the elevator doors parted and she stepped inside.

Would that be the last she saw of Craig? She didn't know. But she'd survived her first interview in this new and exciting country and if nothing else, hopefully gained a little more confidence.

★　★　★

Craig helped himself to a second coffee. Hayley had interviewed well. She was very different from his fiancée. He thought how Leila liked to describe Craig's business as his outback empire, unaware of course, quite how close he sailed to the wind financially.

Maybe he should tell her? But, knowing Leila, she'd run straight to her father, and Craig, who'd already confessed his predicament to Mr Borthwick, preferred to keep this information from her for the moment.

He hated the prospect of being beholden to her father, though he'd walk on hot coals if it would keep Misty Mountain functioning.

The heiress resembled an exquisite china doll, dressed like a model girl and worked part-time in an art gallery. Their families and almost all their friends seemed convinced he and she were made for each other.

Why, then, hadn't they named the big day? Why wouldn't Leila agree to be married at his resort? Except he hoped she was joking when she told him her parents contemplated a guest list of 150. Too many for his resort to cater for, but there were guest houses plus a small hotel in the area. He needed to e-mail Leila a reminder so he could pencil in the date.

Craig pulled out the next applicant's CV. He really wasn't sure about the attractive British girl. He was being truthful when he said he liked her style, and his softer side wanted to give her the chance to work in a foreign country. Hadn't he once been in that position himself?

Hayley had held two important roles since her university days and that said a lot. It must have shaken her up, finding her name on the list of employees facing redundancy.

He still questioned her eagerness to spend time in Australia, given her employment potential back in the UK.

By working for him, she'd be accepting a dramatic drop in salary.

He replaced his cup as the receptionist rang to announce the next candidate.

Standing in the corridor, waiting for the elevator to arrive, he experienced a light-bulb moment. Hayley Collins touched something within him. She mightn't be a sophisticate like Leila, whose movie star looks drew admiring glances, but the British girl possessed a fresh and endearing manner that Craig knew he shouldn't be noticing.

More Than Meets the Eye

Hayley checked her phone again. How long did it take to interview two candidates? Even if Craig Maxwell stopped for lunch, surely he should be in touch by now?

She reached for the TV remote, almost dropping it as her phone rang and trying not to feel disappointed that her friend was calling.

'Hi, Hayley, just thinking about you. How did it go?'

'Better than I'd thought, after the other night.'

'Sounds promising.'

'He thinks I'm over-qualified. Maybe he's afraid to take me on in case I keep looking for something more like my last job.'

'Well, anyone interviewing you would need to do it via Skype, unless you made the four-hour train journey to the city and back.'

'Good point. Let's hope he thinks of that.'

'I'm certain he will. Look, I need to work an extra hour, but I'll pick up something nice for supper. That OK with you?'

'Perfect, and if by some miracle I'm offered this job, I'll take you out to dinner tomorrow night to celebrate.'

'Aw, you sound as though you really want this. I'll keep my fingers crossed for you but I still wish you could find something locally.'

'I might yet. Speak soon.' Hayley rang off, deciding to make herself a cuppa before watching TV.

Once in the kitchen, she heard her mobile phone chime and rushed back at once.

'Hayley speaking.' She hoped she sounded calm.

'Craig Maxwell here. I'm ringing to offer that position we discussed earlier. Do you accept? Or has something else proved more attractive?'

'Oh, my goodness, no! I mean, yes please, I'd like to accept your offer, Craig. Thank you so much.'

His chuckle sent ripples of something she hadn't anticipated travelling down her spine.

'Don't let that enthusiasm fade, Hayley. You sound as though I've just announced your appointment as the new prime minister!'

'Believe me, I'd much prefer the job at Misty Mountain. I'm looking forward to working for you, Craig.'

'Working with me, Hayley. I don't expect to breathe down your neck. I consider you the best of the candidates I've seen and I too look forward to working with you.'

She blinked hard.

'Thank you. Do I need to sign anything?'

'The agency will e-mail you the contract. If you could sign it as a matter of urgency, it'd be much appreciated. I have other applicants I've promised to contact, remember.'

'I won't keep you waiting. I know how I'd feel.'

'Good. Now, we need to firm up your travel arrangements. I'm leaving the day after tomorrow, around eight in the morning, and you're welcome to a ride.

'But if you prefer a more leisurely start, there's a train around noon that'll get you to the nearest station at four o'clock and we'll get someone to meet you.'

Hayley didn't mind an early start and most of her stuff remained unpacked. But could she cope being shut away with her new boss for several hours?

'Have a think,' he continued. 'I'm not great with small talk but there'll be some top countryside to enjoy along the route. Why don't you drop me a text if you decide you can bear to travel with me?'

'I've already thought. Yes, please, I'd appreciate the lift and I'll be down in the foyer by eight.'

'Excellent. This way, it means you're less likely to change your mind.'

She couldn't tell if he was serious. For someone of his background and looks, he had a slight edge of insecurity. Hayley found that surprising and strangely attractive. She dismissed the thought as quickly as it arrived.

'I'll keep checking my e-mails and I promise not to let you down.'

★   ★   ★

True to his word, Craig Maxwell, in a silver four-wheel drive, was outside when Hayley pushed her case through the main entrance. He was out of the vehicle and round to greet her without delay.

'Is this all your luggage?'

'Yes, thank goodness. I'd hate to lug even more stuff around.'

'Let's get it stowed then. There are two coffees in the front. I'm guessing you don't prefer travelling in the back seat?'

'No, thanks. If I did, I'd feel I was starring in 'Driving Miss Daisy'.'

He grinned.

'I can tell you're a morning person. Unlike — er, some folk.'

She settled into her seat while Craig got behind the wheel and pointed to her coffee beaker.

'We can stop for brunch further along. Now, I like the ABC news programme this time of day but we can put music on later. Happy with that?'

'Of course.' Hayley was impressed by his consideration and decided this kind of treatment was a good sign.

She wondered if her training would begin later, or whether she'd be left to relax until tomorrow.

With the city traffic building, Craig needed to concentrate. Hayley watched the queues of vehicles. Whether or not she'd landed on her feet would depend a lot on this man.

Although attractive, presumably with all the advantages of wealth and family, she felt something wasn't right with his world. She shouldn't be thinking this but it was what her instincts dictated.

Hayley soon realised he enjoyed driving. She sneaked a peep at his hands on the wheel, looking away quickly as she imagined how they'd feel cupping her face for a kiss.

Before long, they joined the main highway north and the big car settled into cruising mode, eating up the miles, or kilometres, while she and her new boss remained silent.

Eventually, he spoke.

'You have to be an ideal passenger.'

She glanced sideways.

'I am? In what way?'

'You don't chatter — or fidget. You don't suck in your breath or thump your foot on an imaginary brake pedal. That's what I mean.'

If he only knew . . .

'I feel properly awake,' she replied swiftly, 'now I've had a week of sleeping lying down.'

'Long-haul flying is no-one's favourite pastime.'

'But well worth it to be over here. I'm

really enjoying the chance to soak up this scenery.'

'It gets even better. There'll be glimpses of lakes so maybe some waterfowl. There's cattle around here. Sheep too. A little beyond our stopping place, you'll catch your first sight of that big old mountain in the distance. Are you peckish yet?'

To her surprise, she was. Her appetite recently had gone every which way. Would he pay for her meal? She had plenty of Australian dollars, but didn't want to offend him.

If she had been travelling by train, she'd have purchased a snack and a drink to see her through. Understanding etiquette was bad enough at home sometimes, and here in her temporary new country, she'd just have to play it by ear.

'Here's where we break our journey.' Craig pointed to a three-way junction, with a signboard saying Robbie's Restaurant. He drove into the yard and pulled up beyond the ranch style building.

He came round to open Hayley's door.

'Wash-rooms are that way. I'll see you in the restaurant.'

She headed for the ladies room. Outside again, she pulled her camera from her bag, wanting to photograph the beautiful bronze and cream hens wandering and pecking their way around the forecourt.

As she pushed open the restaurant door, she couldn't help wondering if this was the kind of eating place Craig Maxwell's fiancée enjoyed, then promptly told herself to mind her own business.

She was gazing up at the jumble of rainbow-coloured items hanging from the ceiling when she heard her name called.

'The thing to do is spend a minute or so memorising all those objects then reeling them off.' Craig looked upwards. 'Which one's your favourite?'

'I'm torn between the rickety aeroplane and the purple teddy bear.'

'How about the miniature Elvis between the crocodile and the cross-eyed kangaroo?' His eyes sparkled with mirth and to her dismay she felt that ripple down the spine thing again and needed to remind herself she was there to work for Craig Maxwell, not to fall for him.

What a contrast between this likeable man and the uptight neighbour back in Melbourne. It was as if a switch had been flipped.

'You have a point,' she said.

'Let's sit at the window end so you can keep an eye on the chooks. Do you know what I'm talking about?'

'Craig, you're speaking to someone who's a huge fan of 'Neighbours'. Of course I know. I've just been photographing them.'

He laughed and sat back as the proprietor handed them menus.

'Now, how about something to drink? I'll stick to ginger beer, but they have a great Chardonnay, un-oaked and very delicious if that's your kind of thing.'

'I think I'll have the same as you, please.'

Craig looked up at the proprietor.

'So that's two, please. Hayley, they do a mean pizza here, or you can get an awesome breakfast if you're into eggs, bacon and bangers.'

The proprietor grinned.

'And the rest!'

'It sounds amazing but I'll go with your pizza recommendation.'

The drinks arrived quickly and Craig raised his tankard.

'Here's to a happy experience for you during your stay at Misty Mountain.'

'I'll drink to that.' Hayley took one sip and knew she'd never, ever sampled anything quite so delicious in her life before.

'That tastes amazing! Who needs wine?'

'We're in great wine country hereabouts and at Misty Mountain we pride ourselves on our cellar so don't go helping yourself.'

She hesitated. He sounded stern. But

he reached across and patted her hand.

'I'm joking, Hayley. You'll need to become accustomed to me, I'm afraid.'

She felt her cheeks heat and almost fanned her face with the menu. There was nothing she'd like more than getting better acquainted with her new boss.

She started asking questions about his resort, proving she'd done her homework by researching his website. He obviously appreciated her enthusiasm. Was he a man of different moods? Didn't that make him more interesting?

Hayley almost dozed off as the powerful car ate up the kilometres once they resumed their journey. Although Craig pointed out landmarks, when they reached a section where he fell silent, she felt her eyelids droop and it seemed all too tempting to take forty winks as her dad would call it.

She didn't think she'd drop off, but what was not to like about the contented feeling washing over her?

All at once she could hear someone

speaking. For a moment she couldn't think where she was or who she was with. How embarrassing was that! But the sound of a now familiar male voice roused her.

'We're just twenty minutes away. I thought you might enjoy getting your first view of Misty Mountain, so you need to look to your left when we get around this next bend.'

'Thank you.' Judging by the time displayed on the dashboard, she must have slept for almost an hour but to her intense relief, all seemed fine and she sat up, eager to catch her first glimpse.

'Wow, now that really is a mountain! I was born in a British county famous for its flat landscape but I've spent holidays in Switzerland.'

'How about Wales and Scotland? They're closer to home for you.'

She nodded.

She and Dan had spent a week touring Wales the summer before her world turned upside down. The accident had proved a painful turning point. Life, in that way it sometimes has, threw her a double whammy when unexpected redundancy further hit her confidence.

The need to change her lifestyle had made her contact Jacqui and ask if she could stay with her in Melbourne. Unsure how long she wanted to be overseas, Hayley applied for the twelve months visa covering holiday and employment.

Misty Mountain loomed over the countryside like a huge, hunched up animal surveying its territory — except she couldn't think of any big beast with a purple hide, let alone one as awesome as this giant rock. She glanced at Craig.

'Is Misty Mountain its real name? From its shape, I'd have imagined it being called something more like what it resembles — except I'm not quite sure what that is.'

'Its official name, or geographical name, if you like, is Whale Mountain because of that humped shape, but I'm afraid we locals have nicknamed the old girl 'Misty' and that's what everyone round here calls her. She's often wreathed in mist, you see.'

'It's a more attractive name for your holiday resort than the real one. Well, I think so, anyway.'

'Glad you approve. Back in the day, the resort was known as Whale Mountain but as the years rolled by and my folks had to react to the changing world, someone suggested calling it Misty Mountain and fortunately it turned out to be a good move. Fingers crossed, I might add.'

'It sounds very romantic. Like it's the perfect name to attract couples wanting to get married somewhere really special.' She thought she'd spoken out of turn when a swift glance at his profile showed his tense expression.

'In some people's view, yes, you're right. Sadly, not everyone feels the same nostalgia — the same pull — as I and many of my family and friends do. And I count my staff amongst my friends, Hayley.'

He sounded sincere, but more and more, she felt convinced something was bugging him. Something important that maybe he tried to hide yet found surfacing unexpectedly. But he hardly knew her, so why would he confide in her?

She sensed a wistful longing when he spoke of his home and he'd seemed energised when he collected her earlier, almost like a coiled spring waiting to be released. Longing to be set free from something . . . or someone?

She daren't probe his feelings, nor did she dare look at his capable hands on the steering wheel. She could so easily imagine their owner leaning in to kiss her.

Far safer to watch the mountain disappear from view as Craig left the main road to follow a dirt track, full of ruts and edged with scrubby grass. Now, she couldn't hold back her laughter.

'OK, what's so funny?'

'I was just thinking I wouldn't want

to miss the last bus home and have to stagger along this track in my high heels and party frock.'

'Believe me, it's been done before! On several occasions, guests have missed the coach that takes them to and from the races.

'Drivers always wait a reasonable time but we daren't inconvenience a couple of dozen people for the sake of one or two stragglers.' He glanced across and winked. 'It's strange how it so often turns out to be a twosome, but there you go.'

'That old thing called romance?'

'Yep, I guess so.'

The pause after their conversation seemed to envelope them. She waited for him to ask if she had a boyfriend who might be missing her, but decided Craig must realise she wouldn't have flown so far to find work if there was a Mr Right pining for her at home.

'Very soon you'll have sight of our cottage accommodation.' Hayley noted the pride in his voice. 'A few already have guests staying but we won't linger now. I'll take you to the main house and hand you over to Maria, my right-hand woman.

'She'll answer your questions and show you your quarters. Staff are accommodated in a separate building close by, so you'll have no excuse for being late for work.'

'I can't play the jet lag card?'

He chuckled.

'No way. You've had plenty of time to recover from your flight.'

She couldn't help wondering where the boss stayed. But there was plenty to keep her interested and Hayley looked from side to side as she spotted cute cottages tucked away beside clumps of trees or, in one case, clustered in a row of six.

These looked newer than the rest and appeared to have a dome-shaped attachment one side of each front door.

Hayley queried the domes.

'They're more eco-friendly than the original bathrooms. Each has a walk-in shower plus the usual conveniences.'

'I noticed the eco-friendly mention on your website.'

'We try to move with the times. If we don't keep up, we could be shut up.'

Craig drove on towards a two-storeyed stone building with a short flight of wide steps leading to a front veranda.

'This is the main house. I'll leave Maria to explain its workings. You already know some guests prefer staying here while others go for the laid back cottage life.'

'I can't wait to see everything!'

'Not long now.' He slowed down for traffic humps and parked his car round the back, beside a dark green van bearing the slogan Misty Mountain, in gold script.

'Welcome to my home.'

The look of pride and joy upon his face caused a lump to jump into her throat and she needed to look away, for fear he noticed her emotion. What was going on?

She gave herself a mental shove.

'Thank you so much for the lift, and for the delicious brunch, and most of all for giving me the chance to work at your beautiful resort.'

'You're very welcome. Now, let's get you and your kit inside so you can start to feel at home.'

Heart's Desire

Craig knew Maria would be like a mother hen with a new chick and lost no time in driving straight to the boss's cottage. Everything looked immaculate and in his mini kitchen, all the stainless steel gleamed.

His fridge contained the usual welcome pack and he smiled, noticing someone had tucked a packet of chocolate biscuits in the door shelf.

He switched on his computer, slightly taken aback to find his thoughts drifting to Hayley. The new girl would have plenty on her plate, learning the ropes, but she seemed keen enough.

He pictured the way she tilted her head when concentrating. Today her hair was loose. It was in a ponytail when they first talked from balcony to balcony and for her interview, she'd twisted it in a knot. Today she looked pretty darned gorgeous.

Craig usually got on with British people. He thought they weren't generally as laid back as your average Aussie, but they often displayed a dry sense of humour and a friendliness that mightn't at first be obvious, but which could lead to a long and rewarding acquaintanceship.

While in his early twenties, he'd worked both in London and in a Scottish Highlands hotel and, even a decade or so later, still kept in touch with former colleagues.

The number of messages awaiting attention made him groan. He selected the one from his fiancée. They'd planned to have dinner together last evening, but she insisted on inviting her sister and her sister's latest beau, who was some kind of TV presenter, though Craig couldn't remember which channel.

If he complained, saying they needed more time alone, she always had some excuse. He began reading her message.

This was, after all, the woman with whom he wanted to spend the rest of his life. Wasn't she?

Hey, hope you had a good trip and not too tedious, having that girl along. But you're always so kind to people, Craig. It's not good to get involved with folk you don't know much about. I hope what's-her-name will be OK though it seems you picked the best of a bad bunch.

Leila possessed an unfortunate ability to twist his words to suit herself. Nor was she a people person. She truly didn't realise how spoilt she was.

In your last e-mail you talked about naming a date, Craig continued to read.

Well, brace yourself, honey, because I've decided on a Christmas wedding! What could be more romantic than marrying under a blue sky? I know you'll agree.

Mama and Daddy are all for it and holiday time will be the perfect opportunity for our friends and families to gather.

All we need do is find the right venue, so shall we leave that to my folks? Mama can't wait to get started.

47

By the way, I do mean this Christmas, honey, not next year, and please don't dare complain about short notice. You've been pestering me to name the day for a while, haven't you?

I know you have this crazy notion about getting married at Misty Mountain but, truly, Craig, even you must realise trekking out there won't work!

I know you'll insist your staff know all there is to know about putting on a wedding but my folks set the bar high and I'm a teeny bit frightened they'll throw a wobbly if we insist on getting married in the outback.

Craig read that last paragraph again and put his head in his hands. Misty Mountain was hardly the back of beyond. More importantly, it was his family home.

How many more times would Leila trample over his feelings? Did she want to be his wife or did she hanker after becoming Bride of the Year?

He felt depressed. Annoyed. Betrayed. Reluctantly, he double-checked she really had suggested a Christmas Eve wedding. Peak time of year for his resort!

But might it be worth humouring her, even if holding his wedding over the holiday period would take him away from Misty Mountain? He had not once, since his return from his UK travels, missed working alongside his loyal team over the festive period.

Would backing down to please Leila and her folks encourage her to move into the house down the road where his parents raised him and his little brother?

On their retirement, Craig's folks decided to go travelling and only recently purchased a bungalow that was still being renovated. It had easy access to shops and medical facilities just a short drive from their old home.

It was too much to hope. Leila was too much of a city girl. And she could throw her weight about like one of those Highland caber throwers he'd seen in Scotland. This time, she'd pushed him far enough.

He reached for the telephone. He needed to ask his fiancée one very important question, and if they couldn't reach a compromise, there was only one option. He'd have to call off the whole caboodle and inevitably lose the promised financial support from Leila's father. At that moment, Craig cared neither one way nor the other.

★   ★   ★

'You're a quick learner, Hayley, I'll say that for you.'

Hayley smiled back at Maria.

'There's a lot for you to take in, but I don't think our reservations will be a problem. Just pick up a pen and paper if no-one's around and you're not sure about inputting a new booking.'

'If I'm slow at first, I hope people will forgive me.'

'Hey, I know you'll do fine. And we'll try not to leave you on your own for your first couple of days.'

'Thanks, Maria.'

'Now, how about a quick tour of the main areas before the evening meal? You'll find that a lot more interesting than the office side, I imagine.'

'I'm happy working behind a desk but I can't wait to see the accommodation.'

To her astonishment, Maria bit her lip.

'We're proud of what's been achieved, but you'll notice areas which need updating.'

'That sounds expensive.'

'When it comes to pleasing our guests, the boss is a perfectionist. If you remember that, you won't go far wrong.' She unhooked a key from the nearby board.

'I'll drive and give a running commentary as we go. Tomorrow morning, we'll get you behind the wheel and see how much you've remembered.'

So soon! But Hayley was determined not to fall at the first hurdle.

'No pressure then. But, Maria, if I take a wrong turning, will you throw me out and make me walk back home?'

Maria chuckled.

'You're a star turn, Hayley. I must admit, when I heard Craig was bringing a Brit to join us, I wondered if you might be a bit toffee-nosed. I'm very relieved to find I couldn't have been more wrong.'

'Aw, thanks, Maria. And I couldn't have had a warmer welcome.'

Maria put her head round the door to the other office.

'I'm about to give Hayley the tour, Georgie. Just so you know we're leaving the building. I have my mobile.'

Georgie looked up and smiled.

'Ace, Maria. How's it going, Hayley? You look pretty calm.'

Hayley grinned.

'If I do, it can only be sheer good luck. I'm a bag of nerves inside.'

'Nonsense,' her mentor insisted. 'She's doing fine, Georgie. But we better get going, so see you later.'

Outside, Maria led the way to a dark green estate car. Hayley hopped up alongside Maria who drove slowly down the track, heading for the other side of the estate.

'The converted wool-shed we use for all the big parties is over this way. We'll take a peek at it and you tell me if you can smell fleeces or not.'

'Are you serious?'

'I think it has a distinctive smell. See what you think.'

Maria pulled up at the front then led the way round the side of the barn and unlocked the back door.

'If you think it looks kind of bare and unwelcoming, remember how different it'll be when it's dolled up with fresh flowers and table settings and people wearing their wedding finery.'

Hayley stepped inside and looked around, her gaze lingering on the enormous stone fireplace and giant wicker basket of logs. She turned to Maria.

'That must be fabulous on a chilly

night.' Hayley sniffed. 'I'm not sure if I can recognise the scent of wool but there's a country smell. In a good, homely way, of course.'

Maria nodded.

'Yep, we get cold snaps this time of year, that's for sure. But the log fire adds to the atmosphere and some folk are disappointed when the temperature rockets outside, making a roaring fire as much use as a chocolate teapot.'

'I can imagine.' Hayley followed her guide through the back door. She stood by the vehicle, waiting for Maria to join her, when she noticed dark silhouettes against the landscape.

Horse and rider were galloping along the fence separating Craig's land from that of the neighbouring farmer. Hayley had been briefed about showing consideration to local people, particularly neighbours either side.

'Is that one of the guests, enjoying a ride?' Hayley pointed to the distant horseman.

'Nope, that's the boss putting Flame

through her paces. It doesn't take long before Craig saddles up once he's checked for urgent messages and drunk a cup or three of coffee.' She got behind the wheel again. 'In you get, and I'll take you to the older clutch of cottages. They're not in quite such good nick and they don't have all the equipment upgraded like the modern ones. I guess you saw those earlier, on your way down?'

'Craig pointed them out.'

'Some of our guests have been holidaying here since they were kids and they generally opt to stay in the older cottages but the modern ones have Wi-Fi so a lot of the bright young things coming out of Melbourne for a break from the city like the cottages equipped with the new-fangled stuff.'

They completed their tour and Hayley was advised to get herself unpacked properly and ready for the evening meal.

'Will I meet the rest of the staff then?'

'Pretty well, I think.'

'Craig described his team as loyal and committed to making the business work.'

She watched Maria's face change. Could that smile be just a tad forced?

'That's nice to hear. I just wish he wasn't so under — well, you know, so hard-pushed.'

Hayley wondered if Maria knew what sometimes ruffled Craig's usual demeanour. By the closed look on the older woman's face, the moment had passed and whatever it was Maria wished wasn't about to be confided. What could it all mean?

Craig Maxwell, so popular with his staff, surely couldn't be a tyrant or stingy over working conditions?

So it had to be something Maria felt was wrong or lacking in his business or personal life. Even though Hayley hadn't known her new boss long, she was convinced her feeling that something haunted him wasn't down to an over-active imagination.

* * *

The lovely but immensely spoilt Leila had reached a decision. She responded to his e-mail by telephone, declaring she'd absolutely no intention of leaving the city. What would be the point of making herself miserable? Hadn't Craig taken in any of what she'd been saying over the last few months?

'Leila, sweetheart, if we're to be man and wife, no way can we live in Melbourne when my business is here.'

'I still don't see why you can't commute.'

'Because I don't own a private plane! Are you suggesting I put myself through a horrendous commute on a daily basis?'

Big sigh down the phone.

'Well, of course not, honey. That would be very silly, but surely you could come back Friday night and drive back early Monday?'

'For the millionth time, Leila, Misty Mountain is my livelihood, not just my home. Which part of that do you not understand?

'You know we can get alterations done to the family place to make it more your style.' He'd crossed his fingers at that point, imagining the cost, but she didn't respond.

'You announce you want us to marry at Christmas and yet you seem to think marriage means we can continue like an engaged couple,' he continued, 'instead of becoming man and wife, sharing a life together. Why won't you see things my way?'

That set her off again, attacking his outdated idea, calling him a chauvinist, saying her dad was waiting for his new son-in-law to join the family firm and what was wrong with putting a manager into Misty Mountain or even selling the place?

The two of them could visit his folks now and then — no problem. But her social standing in the city was too important to ignore. She didn't mince her words.

And his stomach churned when she hinted how he'd find life impossible if her father didn't provide the cash injection promised upon their marriage.

'I can't believe your father told you something I considered confidential between me and him.'

'Daddy tells me everything. And you shouldn't have secrets from me.'

'I wonder if you realise how that makes me feel?'

'Rubbish! You're very fortunate to be marrying me, Craig, rather than some little nobody with nothing to offer. Romance is fine in its place but I couldn't bear to do without life's little luxuries. Fortunately for me, Daddy knows it.'

Craig had given her an ultimatum and her response was swift and chilling.

'For goodness' sake, Leila, you're still wearing my ring. Will you marry me and share my life at Misty Mountain or will you not? It's a simple enough question.'

Silence. Then came the answer he'd

been half-anticipating.

'I don't think I can go through with this, honey. I can't move to the back of beyond just for the sake of becoming Mrs Craig Maxwell. I thought you loved me.'

★ ★ ★

Craig patted Flame's shapely neck before handing her over to the man who ran the stable yard. Apart from Flame, Craig kept three horses for guests to ride.

'You certain you don't mind rubbing her down, Ben?'

'Positive, boss. You must have a million things on your plate. It's good to see you back again. We keep the wheels turning while you're away but nothing beats having a Maxwell around.'

Craig felt a surge of happiness, something much needed at that moment.

'Thanks, mate, I'm pleased to be

back, too. Sometimes you can have too much of a good thing.'

'Know what you mean. I enjoy visiting the city but I'd sooner rattle round here in the sticks.'

'That's fortunate for us, Ben.' Craig stroked Flame's nose as the mare whickered, the familiar sound making his owner wish some of the humans in his life were as easygoing as his adored horse.

He walked briskly back along the track to his quarters. He needed to shower and decide whether to eat with his team that evening or, as he'd prefer, to shut himself in his cabin and enjoy food cooked in the big house's kitchen.

He fancied some down time, without having to make conversation, even though he knew his team would probably be disappointed not to hang out with him on his first evening back.

He'd been away several weeks — not necessarily through his own choice. Now, though, he no longer needed to dance to his fiancée's tune.

The broken engagement would sadden many people, especially Leila's folks. His own mum and dad would be more realistic. Looking back, he realised he should have learned a lot from what they didn't say about his engagement rather than what they did.

Deep down, he'd always known Leila wasn't in harmony with the values he held most dear. Equally, she wouldn't thrive away from the city.

He'd been avoiding this significant fact, keeping on working hard, hoping things would sort themselves out.

Again, he asked himself if he loved her enough to give up his favoured lifestyle and toe the line, like the dutiful son-in-law her parents wanted him to be.

He pictured her glossy blonde hair and smooth skin. And she always smelled so heavenly, but why wouldn't she? She had all the salons, spas and top stores at her beck and call.

At that moment, one part of him wanted to jump in his car and turn up at her flat. Take her in his arms. But he knew, after that, he'd be pining for Misty Mountain.

He hardened his heart. So, wedded bliss was no longer on his horizon. Craig knew where his heart's desire truly lay. And that desire, he understood very clearly now, burned far more fiercely than his so-called love for Leila.

Time Stood Still

'More roast veggies, Hayley?'

She shook her head.

'They're delicious, Maria, but I can't eat another thing. That was a lovely meal.'

'You can thank Rusty here for that.' Maria pointed to the tall, auburn-haired man seated further along and talking to Craig, who'd turned up a little late, offering apologies.

'But he'll be gutted if you don't sample his special lemon curd tart.' She winked at Hayley. 'Chef's single, you know.'

Hayley raised her eyebrows, unable to prevent her cheeks from turning pink. But neither could she stop herself from glancing down the table to give the chef another look, catching the eye of her new employer. Craig gave her a brief smile before continuing his conversation.

'You must be tired, Hayley, though I can't say you look it.' Jake, Maria's husband, leaned round his wife. 'No TV to keep you awake . . . wonder how you'll get on with all that peace and quiet.'

'Pretty well, I think. The business couldn't function without an internet connection, though.'

'I have a job keeping up with all that techy stuff.' Jake shook his head. 'I leave it to the wife here. To tell the truth, I'm more at ease with a book in my hand when I get the time.'

Maria addressed the people closest.

'I've appointed Hayley as our technology whizz from now on.' She patted Hayley's hand. 'I could do with a refresher course some time.'

'That'll depend on how long it takes me to learn your systems, I suppose,' Hayley said. She clenched both fists in her lap while trying to appear composed.

'I'd better warn you, Maria's putting

me in the driver's seat tomorrow, Jake, so you might find it helpful to scatter some red for danger signs around.'

'You'll be fine, just you wait and see. My Maria's got more patience in her little finger than I have in the whole of my body.'

Hayley smiled but her attention was drawn to a movement at the other end of the table. Rusty had gone to fetch dessert and one of the younger girls was clearing away dishes.

She jumped as Craig pulled out the empty chair opposite.

'Mind if I join you?'

It had taken much soul-searching before he could force himself into the shower and into blue denims and black sweatshirt ready to face his employees.

But this was his life and he'd chosen to remain single rather than bow to his former fiancée's wishes. That would have been turning his back on his heritage, insulting those before him who, like his great-grandfather George Maxwell, started out by farming the land on which the resort stood.

His descendants had followed his example, adapting and improving. The financial dilemma Craig faced was nothing compared with the hardships great-grandpa George must have had, battling weather and stubborn land, without today's technology.

But his parents were no longer the driving force and the people around him now were not only his responsibility but his family, a thought that both pleased and saddened him, given his not so bright prospects.

'How are these two treating you, Hayley? You're not about to turn tail and head back to the city, I hope?'

'What a thing to say, boss!' Maria put on a stern face. 'We haven't even had a chance to send the girl out for a roo's tail yet.'

Hayley looked from one to the other but saw how Jake was finding difficulty in keeping a straight face.

'Ah, is this an in-house joke? Like at home, back in the day, a new employee would be sent out to buy half a pound of scruples or a can of elbow grease?'

'She's too sharp to be taken in. Good on you, girl.' Jake looked appreciatively at the large slice of lemon tart before him. 'You're surely not going to miss out on this, Hayley?'

The dessert looked scrumptious. Rusty was gazing at her and she didn't wish to offend the chef on her first night. Her heart flip-flopped behind her ribcage as someone rode to the rescue.

'I'll go halves with you, Hayley. Is that OK?' Craig nodded at his chef. 'Much too good to miss, Rusty, but Hayley and I put away a substantial brunch on the way here so please forgive us for not managing the full whack this time.'

'It's paradise on a plate, that's for sure,' Maria said, while those around nodded agreement.

Hayley was conscious of Craig watching as she cut into her share of the crumbly pastry and luscious lemon topping and for a moment she forgot anyone else was in the room.

He must have realised what was happening because, as she dragged herself away from inappropriate thoughts, he met her gaze. Pull yourself together, she scolded herself.

To her relief, Jake suddenly spoke.

'What time do you want to meet up tomorrow, boss? I've been making notes of stuff I need to talk to you about.' Jake looked across at Craig.

'How about eleven o'clock in my office? I'll have done my walkabout by then.'

'Let's hope you find everything in order.'

'I'd be surprised not to.' Craig put down his spoon.

'How about if Hayley accompanies you, boss?' Maria said. 'It might be good for her to see how you check on details, the kind of things you set store by. Just a suggestion,' she added hastily.

Craig drained his water glass and propped his chin in his hands.

'It's not a bad idea. What if we meet in reception at eight-thirty sharp? We'll drive, in case you were wondering.'

'I'll be ready.'

'I'm expecting Hayley's uniforms to be delivered tomorrow,' Maria chimed in, 'but not until after lunch, so that works well. I'd prefer to make sure they fit before accepting the order.'

'That's settled, then.' Craig got to his feet. 'Now, I've enjoyed your company, guys, but if you'll excuse me, I'm calling it a day. I wish you all a very good night.'

Next morning, Hayley arrived at reception with mixed feelings. This job obviously had many different aspects. She'd expected that, of course. Welcomed it, even if she wondered whether she could cope with everything as her employer wished.

But there was no time for the jitters, because Craig pushed open the outer door at precisely 29 minutes past eight.

'All set?'

'You bet!' She may as well sound

cheerful and positive, even if nervousness plagued her.

What business did she have thinking she could hold down a job so different from her former one? Also, she was a scarily long way from home. That fact was only just starting to sink in.

'I hope I'm not rushing you?'

He looked concerned. He was so nice, so unlike the man she'd first perceived him to be. She desperately needed to chase off her early morning butterflies.

'I'm fine, thanks, but still having that new-girl feeling and hoping I can do a good job. With such a great team, you don't need passengers.'

They were standing beside his car. He took her by the shoulders but so very gently, she felt like marshmallow melting in sunshine as those big, warm hands held her.

'Cut yourself some slack, Hayley, because you've made an excellent start. I heard people saying as much last night. So, go with the flow and don't rush things. We're in this together, you and me.' He released her. 'D'you fancy a turn at the wheel?'

Could she do this?

'OK. You never know, I might even manage to impress Maria when it's her turn to be my passenger.'

'Brilliant.' He handed her the car key. 'I'll navigate.'

It wasn't quite so easy once inside the car. One whiff of his heavenly after-shave and she found it difficult to figure out how to get going. What had she let herself in for?

'You mightn't have driven an automatic before?'

'Actually, I haven't, but it can't be that difficult, surely?'

Craig's laughter filled the car.

'I love your positive attitude. Now, are you up for this? I can talk you through.'

Why did she suddenly find difficulty in breathing?

'OK, I promise to do exactly what you say.' She hoped her guardian angel was on duty.

She tried hard to concentrate while he gave basic instructions. Should she confess what happened that terrible day when Dan had been at the wheel? No way. She daren't do anything to cause Craig to question her ability. Or to pity her.

'This isn't a ceremonial procession,' he said after a while.

'I'm finding it weird, not having to use both feet to control the car.' The fib came easily. At least, with so much to think about, the slight tension she'd sensed between them had disappeared.

He asked her to pull up at a vacant cottage, one of the newer ones.

'We have guests arriving later so we should find almost everything in place.' He held out a key. 'How about you go first and pretend you've booked in. Give me your first impressions.'

They walked up to the porch. The key turned easily and Hayley pushed open the door. A beam of sunshine shone on a polished wood table in the living room. She could smell lavender wax polish. Nice.

'Where do you go first?'

She thought for a moment.

'I've been driving a long time and I can't wait to get unpacked and settled but I need to visit the bathroom.' To her left she noticed an interior door. 'Is it through there?'

'Spot on.'

Hayley was met by gleaming surfaces, snowy white towels and a fresh aroma. A set of upmarket toiletries stood either side of the oval wash basin and she picked up a bottle of shampoo to find it contained comfrey. Another contained chamomile. All very much in tune with the environment. She checked out the walk-in shower, unsurprised when she found nothing to criticise.

'Fabulous toiletries! And everything gleams.'

'What next?'

'The bedroom, I think.' She wondered if he'd follow, to watch her reaction.

But he turned away, taking five or six strides to stand in front of the window. Hands in his jeans pockets, he stared out at the landscape while she suddenly felt an urge to go across and give him a hug.

She needed to get a grip. Being around this man made her feel as though attracted by a magnet and struggling to resist its pull.

She focused on her surroundings. Again, everything looked perfect. Immaculate white linen, open-front clothes closet with plenty of hangers and an enormous double bed. Everything spelled comfort and luxury. She rejoined him in the mini kitchen.

'All well?'

'Very well indeed,' she said. 'I'd be thrilled to walk into that room if I'd booked in.'

'Excellent. Now, come check out the fridge and don't be afraid to comment.'

She scanned the shelves and door rack.

'Locally produced butter and eggs.

No milk though I imagine that'll be delivered later. We're here ahead of normal check-in time so I wouldn't expect to find the full welcome pack.'

'Quite right,' he said. 'What do you think of all this?' He pulled apart the big doors concealing domestic equipment.

'Wow, it's amazing how much you can fit in there. They even get an electric frying pan.'

'That's so they can cook their own eggs and bacon without having to get dressed and go over to the main house.'

'And chef puts on brunch for those who prefer being waited on.'

Craig nodded.

'I noticed you seemed to be getting on well with him last night. Rusty's a sociable kind of guy, isn't he?'

She bit her lip. Again, there was something in Craig's tone she couldn't get her head around.

'I tried to talk to as many people as possible.'

'Understood.'

Hayley could stand it no longer.

'Forgive me if I'm putting my foot in it. I hardly know you but I get the feeling something's bothering you.' She wasn't arrogant enough to think he might be in the least jealous of her tentative friendship with his chef, yet, something jarred.

Already, she cared about Craig Maxwell in a way she shouldn't.

He stepped closer. She saw a spark of something in his gaze. Curiosity? Regret? Or something else?

He spread his hands.

'You don't stand on ceremony, do you? Anyone would think you were an Aussie!' The remark did the trick. She chuckled and so did he.

'Let's say personal relationships are causing me difficulties just now. I apologise if I'm being less than professional, Hayley.'

His eyes, those gorgeous eyes, were challenging her. What did this man want? Sympathy? A shoulder to cry on? Something more powerful? But she daren't even dream of such things. Craig wasn't only spoken for, he was way out of her league.

Yet, she knew she'd remember this moment as one when time appeared to stand still. Briefly she closed her eyes and when she forced them open again, she felt sure he'd inched closer.

He reached out a hand. Withdrew it at once. She struggled not to reach out too, aware that could only lead to embarrassment for both of them.

And Hayley daren't risk jeopardising not only this precious job but also her fragile self-esteem.

The chime of his mobile phone broke the spell. Hayley turned away to allow him privacy. On her way to the door, she couldn't help overhearing.

'I thought we had no further reason to communicate!' Craig exclaimed. Yet, when he joined her outside and locked up the cottage, he seemed not to have a care in the world.

'OK,' he said, 'we'll check one of the original two-bedroom cottages now.

Then we'll go back and grab a coffee before Maria throws you into reception. That is, if you can manage to get this vehicle up and running again.'

'I'll take that as a joke, Mr Maxwell.' He'd never know how close to the truth he was.

'I rather enjoy being chauffeured for a change,' he replied. 'But I'd hate to have you drive me if I needed to catch a train.'

If Ever a Man Needed Comfort...

'Now you look the business.'

'It's not a bad fit, is it?' Hayley did a twirl before the mirror in Maria's office. 'Who chose the coffee and cream colour scheme?'

'The boss — a couple of years back.'

'I liked the effect as soon as I saw you and Georgie in your uniforms. That stripy cravat against the cream blouse and darker skirt works well.'

'Glad you agree, Now, I'm off to take some clothes for dry cleaning and pick up a couple of magazines for a guest who can't survive without her celebrity fix.' She shook her head. 'To think we pride ourselves on creating a peaceful haven, away from it all. Do you need anything?'

'I don't think so, thanks. You're not

taking Georgie, I hope?'

'Georgie will be here. If you can proof-read those menus while I'm gone, it'll be much appreciated. Rusty may cook like an angel but he certainly has no knack for writing plain English.' Maria clicked her fingers.

'I almost forgot to say, the boss doesn't want his ex-fiancée put through if she calls on the land line. Leila Borthwick is the name and it's no use asking what's going on because I haven't a clue.' Maria raised her eyebrows heavenwards and hurried out.

Hayley wondered what caused this break-up between Craig and his bride-to-be. He'd sounded uptight when taking that call at the cottage, yet he was completely calm afterwards. The man was a mystery. The phone rang not long after Maria drove away.

'Misty Mountain Resort. Good after-noon.' Hayley slid her chair closer to the computer.

'I'd like to speak to the owner.'

Hayley almost requested the magic word. The woman sounded self-assured and came across as if she resented talking to an underling.

'I'll check if Mr Maxwell's in. May I ask who's calling, please?'

'The name's Vanessa Grey and I can assure you, he wouldn't want me to be kept waiting.'

'Hold the line, please.' Hayley used her crispest English accent. She rang Craig's office extension. No reply. Back to her caller, she apologised for being unable to put her through.

'May I take a message? Mr Maxwell's probably out on the estate somewhere.'

'Can't you page him?'

'Excuse me, but is this a personal or business call?'

'Hayley? I'm back. Someone wanting me?'

'One moment, please.' Hayley put the call on hold. 'Vanessa Grey's asking for you.'

'Really? That's my darling godmama. I wonder what the old bird wants!'

Hayley smothered a giggle.

'So will you take it in your office?'

'Yeah, I'd better, in case she doesn't give me my pocket money next time we meet!' He disappeared into his office, closing the door behind him.

Hayley waited until the boss picked up his phone. As she resumed her proof-reading, she noticed Craig's voice becoming louder. Her employer's personal life wasn't her concern, but she couldn't help wonder what Vanessa Grey had done to upset him.

When the other line rang, Hayley answered quickly and dealt with an inquiry about a small wedding celebration.

She enjoyed describing the peaceful country location and the facilities, while hoping the caller couldn't detect Craig's high level decibels in the background.

She'd barely put down the phone when Craig's door burst open.

'Tell me something, please! What the heck did she say to persuade you to put her through? I thought I made it clear to Maria that I wasn't to be troubled by calls from Ms Borthwick.'

Hayley froze.

'The caller introduced herself as Vanessa Grey. With respect. I did tell you when you asked who was calling. If Ms Borthwick had given me her real name, of course I wouldn't have put her through, considering Maria gave me your instructions.'

Knowing how she'd been conned, Hayley wasn't amused by Craig's high-handed attitude.

His face softened.

'Of course. I lost it for a minute there. No way are you to blame, Hayley. I apologise for bawling you out. Leila's my problem and I've no right to expect my staff to shield me.'

'That's OK. It's unfortunate Maria wasn't still here, isn't it? I presume she'd have recognised the voice.'

He scowled.

'Maybe. If Leila calls again, I'll speak to her.'

'I'm sorry if things aren't going well between you and your fiancée.'

'My ex-fiancée, to be accurate, as I've ended my engagement. It won't be long before everyone knows.'

Hayley gazed up at her boss, unsure what else to say. Luckily, he changed the subject.

'I've just noticed you're wearing your new uniform. It suits you.'

Before she could thank him, the phone rang again and he turned away, going out into the heat of the day.

She heard his engine start up. Perhaps he'd head for the stables, because, if ever a man needed comfort and familiarity, that man was Craig Maxwell.

★　★　★

'I've done something awful.'

Maria eyed her new colleague.

'Have you murdered a guest? Locked the boss in the cellar and thrown away the key?'

85

Despite her anxiety, Hayley couldn't help laughing.

'Neither of those things but I put a call through that I shouldn't have.'

Maria hung up the car key.

'Don't get so stressed, Hayley. I imagine it was Leila ringing for Craig? So he had to talk to her? That doesn't constitute a hanging offence.'

'He hit the roof but he apologised and agreed it wasn't my fault. She introduced herself as Vanessa Grey and when I told him who was calling he joked that he'd better talk to her in case she stopped his pocket money — something like that, anyway.'

'Aha, he thought his godmother was on the line? That was a cunning trick — I can't believe the heiress would stoop so low. I hope she got a telling off for her sins.'

'I've no idea. Anyway, I'll survive, and Craig said, if Ms Borthwick rings again, he'll speak to her.'

'A wise decision. Anything else?'

'I answered an inquiry about holding

a wedding. The date was free so I've pencilled in the booking and written down contact details so I can consult with you about a quotation.'

'We'll deal with that in a minute. So, has Craig gone walkabout?'

'I heard him drive away.'

'I'd bet my last dollar he's at the stables. That's where he always goes when he wants to think something through.'

Hayley didn't confess she'd already thought of that.

'Do you reckon I should follow him? Apologise again?'

'You've nothing to apologise for. You were duped by a manipulative woman. I know I shouldn't say this but I think it's a good thing he's cut loose. I almost jumped for joy when he gave me the news. I know that sounds awful but I totally mean it, though I didn't say so, obviously.'

'He seemed a bit on edge when he took a call while we were out earlier. He told me he was having problems with personal stuff so it could've been her ringing then.' She hesitated. 'You said heiress. Is Ms Borthwick really worth a fortune?'

★ ★ ★

Not for the first time, Craig sensed Flame knew something bothered him. His beautiful mare was trotting steadily down a track where trees either side bent their branches to create a shady arched walkway.

He didn't intend keeping the horse out for long and although the temperature had rocketed, he knew neither he nor Flame would come to any harm, as long as he played safe.

Wouldn't it be great if he could do that with his personal relationships? Not that he'd enjoyed too many of those. Now, looking back at their two years together, he recognised his failure to heed more warning signs than you'd find on a stretch of shark-infested coastline.

He'd been infatuated. Blind to lovely Leila's faults. And when she didn't get her way, his former fiancée lost no time in showing her not-so-lovely side.

Gently, he smoothed Flame's mane. He felt calmer and knew he must return to the office and work on the figures he needed when he next visited his bank.

He guided Flame into a U-turn and she trotted back along the way they'd come, until he brought her to a halt where the shady avenue ended.

Craig dismounted and led her towards the stables, raising his free hand in appreciation as a large black limo glided slowly past. That would be guests arriving to claim their cottage.

He didn't recognise the vehicle but anyone who minded their manners when overtaking a horse had to be a good guy in Craig's book.

He watched the car drive towards the main house and park to one side of the forecourt. A man who looked to be heading for fifty but fit with it, got from behind the wheel and stretched his tall frame.

When his companion left the vehicle, Craig sucked in his breath but continued on his way. Flame was his first priority.

Dramatic Showdown

Hayley glanced up as the door opened and a tall man stood back, allowing his companion to enter. The elegant blonde woman gave Hayley a condescending glance.

'We're here to see Mr Maxwell.'

'Is this a business appointment?' Hayley glanced at the open diary. 'I don't see anything marked in for this morning.'

'That's probably because we've been far too busy to bother with petty details.' The visitor removed her sun hat, shook back her golden curls and nodded towards the boss's office door.

'Maybe we should wait in Mr Maxwell's office while you alert him. I imagine he has his mobile phone on him, don't you?'

Hayley bristled, loathing that feeling of being patronised. But, she had no idea what relationship existed between the couple and her boss, so wouldn't dream of upsetting them.

'May we offer you some refreshment while I contact Mr Maxwell?' Hayley's hospitality didn't extend to allowing them into Craig's inner sanctum. What if she was dealing with a couple of con artists?

'A glass of water would be very welcome,' the blonde said, not even bothering to look at Hayley.

In her turn, Hayley felt a jolt of triumph as the woman and her escort sat down on the chintz-covered settee. She went through to the other office and reached into the fridge for a large glass bottle of water, sealed with an old-fashioned stopper.

Georgie looked up.

'The boss has visitors,' Hayley said.

'Is he on his way?'

'Not unless he's psychic.'

Georgie spluttered.

'You crack me up, you really do!'

'I'm about to call his mobile. That

pair have no appointment and I'd like to find out more about them before I bother Craig.'

'Are you always like this? Like what's her name — Miss Maple, is it?'

'Miss Marple? Ha! Not especially. It's just that I have an uneasy feeling about these two.' She gasped. 'I clean forgot to take their names. What a muppet!'

'Let me take the water through. I'll say you're having trouble locating the boss, then check what their names are.'

'Thanks, Georgie.'

But when her colleague returned and closed the connecting door, Hayley received a shock.

'Cripes, that's only Craig's fiancée you're entertaining. I've no idea who's with her, but something must be up if the heiress has driven from the city!'

'So she's Leila Borthwick? That's twice I've heard her referred to as the heiress.'

'Her family's loaded. Craig's isn't.'

'But I only spoke to her on the phone a while ago. The boss will blow a gasket . . . ' Hayley hesitated. The little she knew about Craig's personal affairs came via Maria and now he'd confided his engagement was ended, no way would she risk being accused of gossiping.

'He's what?'

'He's, erm, gone for a ride, I think. Maria says he enjoys his quiet time with Flame.'

'Sure, but I guess he'll be pleased to see his bride-to-be. It's so romantic, turning up to surprise him like this!'

Hayley picked up the office mobile to call Craig's number. He had, after all, stated he'd deal with Leila, if she called again, though he wouldn't be expecting a personal visit.

Craig answered at once. She heard those dark chocolate tones and couldn't help wishing for something she shouldn't.

'I see we have company,' Craig said. 'No need to explain.'

'So you know who's arrived?'

'The female half of the duo's known

to me, yes. The car passed Flame and me just now. I assume they're waiting?'

'Sitting in reception, drinking iced water.'

'And you haven't shown them into my office?' He sounded amused.

'No way. They could've been a couple of confidence tricksters and I didn't ask their names in case they gave false ones. Georgie recognised Ms Borthwick.'

Craig seemed to be having a coughing fit and she held the phone away from her ear before listening to his response.

'I'll be five minutes.'

Hayley sauntered over to the visitors. 'Mr Maxwell will be here very soon.'

The heiress opened her mouth to speak, but to Hayley's relief, the phone rang and she was busy confirming a booking when Craig, looking totally laid back, entered reception. Without cracking even the ghost of a smile, he beckoned the heiress and her friend into his office.

'To what do I owe this unexpected pleasure?' Remembering his manners, Craig held out his hand to Leila's companion. 'Craig Maxwell. Pleased to meet you.'

'Steven Slessor. My friends call me Steve.'

'Please sit down, Mr Slessor.'

Leila was already seated by the window. She looked, Craig thought, extremely smug. And, strangely, he wasn't feeling that frisson of excitement so familiar whenever near her. He realised he was no longer attracted by her glamour, even though she'd crossed her perfect, honey-gold legs to display tanned thighs.

'What can I do for you?'

Steven Slessor opened a blue folder.

'I have an interesting proposition for you, Mr Maxwell.'

'Is that so?' Craig settled into the black leather executive chair he found so uncomfortable. Leila had ordered it as a surprise, but now he could donate the despised object to charity and buy something more to his liking.

'I have a client wishing to acquire your business.'

'Really.' Craig's tone was flat.

Mr Slessor nodded.

'This is a serious proposition, Mr Maxwell.'

'Is that so, Mr Slessor? Well, what you describe as my business is also my home. My family have run this beautiful estate for more than two centuries. It's not something to be parcelled up and sold off for building. I take it you're a property consultant?'

Steven Slessor nodded.

'Yes, sir.' He handed Craig a sheet of paper. 'That sum of money is an initial offer, taking into account the somewhat inconvenient location. In my profes-sional view, it's a very generous bid and one you'd do well to consider, Mr Maxwell.

'Forgive me for saying so, but as things stand with you, I recommend you don't allow sentiment to cloud your judgement.'

Craig, shaking with rage, pushed back the sheet of paper without even glancing at it.

'I'm not interested and I'll thank you to keep your views to yourself.' He addressed his former fiancée for the first time. 'I take it you put your friend here up to this idiotic farce?'

Leila pouted.

'But it's a fantastic opportunity, darling. You can wave goodbye to all your money problems and come back to the city. Come back to me.'

Craig stared at her until she dropped her gaze and studied her turquoise varnished fingernails, her lips a narrow line.

He rose and walked to the door.

'I won't take up any more of your valuable time, Mr Slessor. Let me see you out.'

'But, darling, aren't you going to put us up overnight?' Leila's eyes were like Bambi's. 'The three of us can chat over one of Rusty's delicious dinners and crack open a bottle of wine. You're tired and upset. You need time to relax so you can think straight. I know you so well, honey.'

'Do you, Leila? Do you really? In that case you should know I've no intention of selling the business I love. I'm disgusted with you. Now, goodbye both.'

He waited until he heard Slessor mutter something to Leila, who stomped past Craig, her high-heeled sandals clicking on the parquet floor.

'I can't believe you could be so stupid! So pig-headed!' Her voice had lost its sultry purr. 'You'll regret this. You see if you don't!'

'I very much doubt it, Leila. Thanks for dropping by. I hope you have a good life.'

Hearing this, Hayley uttered a silent cheer. Way to go, Craig Maxwell! But she wondered why Leila had come all this way, bringing the older man with her. Was he her father?

Hayley kept her head down as her boss sauntered over to the window, presumably watching the limo pull away. She wondered if the pair would drive straight back to Melbourne. Leila must be incandescent over Craig's swift dismissal, so probably wouldn't make too charming a travel companion.

Craig turned round.

'I guess you heard something of that?'

'Only the shouty bits at the end.'

'I'm sorry.'

'You don't need to apologise. Anyone would think you were British.'

He turned and gave her a wry smile.

'Anyway, you weren't the one doing the shouting.'

He hesitated.

'I guess it's common knowledge round here my engagement's at an end and I'm the baddie?'

She chose her words carefully.

'I don't think so but I imagine Maria must know. You did tell her you didn't want to speak to Miss Borthwick should she phone.' No way would she let him know Maria had been a tad indiscreet.

He nodded.

'I told her but she'd have guessed anyway. Maria knows more about me than I do.'

'You sounded very certain.'

'I'm certain all right.' He moved a little closer. 'Have you ever been blinded by love, Hayley? Or something we assume is love, but turns out not to be?'

Heat flooded her face. Was she blinded by love for him? Certainly she'd never felt quite like this before.

And, Dan — that was a painful episode she'd rather forget. She'd cried buckets when he confessed he no longer wanted her in his life. Why would she risk feeling the sting of rejection again?

'You don't have to answer.' Craig's voice was gentle. 'I just turned down the chance to sell this estate.' He quickly changed the subject. 'I know you realise why.'

She nodded.

'I need to keep a keen eye on my finances, that's for sure, but if business keeps improving, I shall breathe more easily. Thanks for fitting in and cottoning on to the job so quickly.'

'I love being here. May I say something?'

'Be my guest.'

'I couldn't help hearing how you stood up, not only for your livelihood, but your home, too. Gosh, I'm sorry, Craig — I have no business commenting.'

He shook his head.

'Now it's my turn to say don't apologise. I never proposed to Leila simply to get my hands on her father's moneybags. To be honest, I had other attributes in mind at the time.' He paused.

'Why, Hayley Collins, I do believe you're blushing. How about I go and make us a pot of traditional English tea? I reckon you and Georgie deserve it.'

Jealous Guy

Hayley had looked forward to helping prepare for a wedding. To her delight, flicking through the bookings a few days after Leila's visit, she noticed almost every cottage was booked for the following Thursday through to Sunday, flagged as a wedding party. By breakfast-time the day the guests were due and Hayley was fizzing with excitement.

Maria teased her.

'You're like a child wanting to see what Santa's brought!'

'I can't wait to see everything coming together.'

'These next few days will really test your skills. The boss did explain you might find yourself lending a hand wherever needed?'

'He did. So, where will I be working this morning?'

'I've put you down to prepare the bridal cottage.'

Hayley had done her share of chambermaid duties but this time, she'd be using the finest quality bed linen, luxurious towels and upmarket toiletries.

'Will I be on my own?'

'I'll make sure you have everything you need then move on to other tasks,' Maria said. 'The flowers will arrive early tomorrow morning but we'll talk about final touches later. What we want from you, Hayley is perfection — or as near as you can get.

'We aim to make their stay memorable for all the right reasons.' She checked her watch.' We'll get cracking straight after breakfast. Starting early should mean you don't end up in a tizzy.'

★ ★ ★

Much to Hayley's relief, Maria took the wheel. When she pulled up opposite the bridal cottage they got out.

'How long have you been with us now?' Maria asked. 'It feels like for ever.'

'Thanks — I think! It's actually just over a month.'

'Have you done much driving with the boss?'

Hayley pulled the cottage key from her pocket.

'Let's just say he didn't jump from the car! I'll unlock, shall I?'

'Please. I'll bring the pack of bed linen first.'

Minutes later, Hayley had all she needed.

'You happy for me to scarper?' Maria asked.

'Of course. I'll call Georgie if I have any queries.'

'I'll get off to the wool-shed, then. When you've done, just come down and make yourself a cuppa before I find you another job.'

'Thanks, Maria.'

Left alone, she made up the bed with finest quality cotton sheets and struggled a bit with the giant but lightweight duvet. A scattering of palest grey satin boudoir pillows added the finishing touch to the snowy nest.

In the bathroom, she discovered there was such a thing as bath caviar, not to mention green seaweed bath fizz. She arranged miniature bottles of toiletries and left plenty of towels.

Working to ensure the couple's every need was met sent Hayley's imagination into overdrive. She couldn't help wondering how it would be to spend a night in the cottage with the man of her dreams, even though she knew someone like Craig Maxwell would never in a million years fall in love with someone like her.

She was locking the door when a voice from nowhere made her jump.

'Are you OK, Hayley?' Craig stood beside his car, his expression puzzled.

'I'm fine. Sorry, am I running late?'

'Nope. I've been working down the row, checking log baskets. This Australian spring of ours can be a bit stroppy and the log burners might be needed over the next few evenings.'

'Well, you don't need to check this one. I already made sure the basket was well-stocked.'

He whistled.

'So the only thing left for me to carry over the threshold is you?'

She stared at him, her heart almost leaping from her chest. What was he playing at? The quip he appeared to find so humorous sent her head spinning. It was dangerously close to the fantasy scenario recently playing out in her head. She checked again she'd locked the door, turning her back on him.

'Hayley?'

She wanted to ignore him but realised how stupid that would be. Her boss had made a harmless joke without realising how she felt about him.

If she didn't take care, the penny would drop and her life would become miserable. He'd be uncertain how to talk to her. The easy fellowship between them would vanish.

He walked right up to her. So close, she need only reach up her hand to touch his cheek. She still stood in front of the cottage so couldn't take even one step back from this very clear and present danger.

'I'm sorry for that ridiculous remark. Sometimes I lose all sense of tact and diplomacy.'

'Let's forget it, shall we? I'd better get on now, otherwise Maria will wonder where I am.'

He seemed reluctant to let her go.

'Let me give you a lift. I have to drive into town so it's hardly out of my way.'

It seemed churlish not to accept but they didn't speak while he drove the short distance to the wool-shed.

*   *   *

Craig was convinced Hayley had issues about marriage, so was fighting personal demons. Maybe she too had experienced the trauma of a broken engagement. Such a lovely young woman couldn't have reached the age of twenty-three without encountering some sort of romantic drama.

He'd love to date her. But he'd made it a rule to avoid becoming emotionally involved with anyone on his staff. And, of course, once he began seeing Leila, no-one else mattered. Anyway, Hayley probably wouldn't be interested in a man who'd so recently ended a relationship.

Craig drove back to the main house to check progress in the kitchen. Next, he had to pick up some items down town but most important of all, he needed to banish Hayley from his thoughts.

Maybe it wouldn't be a bad thing if she started dating Rusty. But as soon as that idea occurred to him, and he pictured the two of them together, Craig couldn't stop himself from thumping his fist on the steering wheel.

★   ★   ★

By late afternoon, Hayley thought the former shearing shed resembled fairy land. Two long rows of tables, draped with white linen, were set with silver-edged paper napkins, name cards, elegant crockery and silver cutlery, while crystal glasses glistened at every place setting.

Wedding favours and fresh floral arrangements would be added next day, ready for the late afternoon feast.

Strings of fairy lights suspended from the rafters had been checked and switched off again. An enormous log fire was ready to light should the evening prove chilly, though Hayley imagined food, drink and dancing would soon make everyone forget the gloomy evening weather forecast. A band was due to arrive next morning and they'd play at the ceremony and for dancing later.

Hayley was walking down the outer side of the second table, examining each place setting, when she saw Rusty arrive.

Maria caught her eye.

'He likes to check we've put out the right cutlery for his menu.' She shrugged. 'He knows we'd never let him down but will he listen?'

Hayley chuckled.

'Shall I ask if I've done the right thing by putting out chopsticks for the guests to eat their main meal with?'

Maria's eyes widened.

'You little devil! Well, on your own head be it, girl.'

Hayley started walking towards the front of the big barn. Rusty noticed her and waved.

'Hi, gorgeous!'

Hayley called out her question. The chef strode towards her, but not without giving the cutlery a hard stare to make sure she really hadn't carried out what she claimed. She backed away from him, still laughing.

'You don't get away that easy,' he called. Moments later he had her in a fireman's lift.

'Hey, just because you're bigger than

111

me!' Hayley struggled without success.

That scene greeted the boss as he came through the main entrance but Craig soon realised no-one had noticed him. Certainly neither Rusty nor Hayley was looking his way, so engrossed they seemed with one another. But as he took in the scene, wondering what prompted the high jinks, the chef put Hayley down on both feet again.

'Either I get a kiss or you get to eat your supper with chopsticks,' Rusty teased.

'I'm useless with chopsticks. What's for supper?' Hayley didn't struggle to escape, but nor did she opt to kiss him.

'There's a vat of chicken gumbo simmering back in the kitchen,' Rusty said.

Craig watched as Hayley stood on tiptoe to give the chef a kiss. Not a passionate one but enough to make Craig turn round and head out. He needed a moment to compose his feelings, that was all.

But, Maria caught the boss's eye as he walked towards the door and he knew his right hand woman and trusted friend had read his face. And, as he once told Hayley, Maria knew him better than he knew himself.

A Walk in the Moonlight

Hayley neither heard the pastor's words, nor the responses from the young woman and man before him, though their expressions told the story unfolding beneath a cornflower blue sky.

She was observing from the main house, while rows of guests, seated on white chairs tied with pale grey and mauve ribbons, enjoyed the ceremony.

Hayley had seen the bride before she made that last walk as a single woman, across the lawn to join her groom. She admired the slender white lace dress and posy of palest pink roses and white gardenias while the bride's father helped his daughter descend the three steps down from the veranda and the musicians played 'What A Wonderful World'.

Hayley jumped as Craig appeared

and whispered in her ear.

'Can't beat the old songs!'

She was puzzled when he squeezed her elbow in a comforting gesture, but he didn't linger and Hayley headed back to the office.

Maria joined her.

'Did all go well? No last minute shocks like in 'Four Weddings And A Funeral'? Though I have to say I love that movie.'

'Me too. I like happy endings.'

'But surely a happy ending is merely the beginning for all newlyweds?'

'Of course. The really hard stuff begins now.'

Maria gave her a shrewd look.

'Dare I ask if you speak from experience?'

'I've never been married or even engaged, but so many relationships break up, marriage can't possibly be one long honeymoon.'

'When you meet Mr Right, you'll see marriage differently.' Maria reached for a box of brochures.

'Maybe there is no Mr Right for me. Why should I expect there to be?'

'You're young, Hayley. There's someone out there waiting for you, you bet your boots! Don't you ever daydream about meeting someone?'

Hayley thought carefully. The question was so intensely personal yet she knew her mentor wasn't prying.

'I suppose most of us hope to meet someone who'll love us and who we can love back. And I don't mean only attractive couples like those two who've just got married. I'm not knocking them but love doesn't always come with blue skies and designer outfits, does it?

'Love comes in many different forms. Sometimes two of the most unlikely people can form a beautiful relationship.'

* * *

Through the half-open door of his office, Craig tuned into the conversation the moment he heard Hayley state

116

her views. He just knew it! She was nursing a broken heart, yet here she was, deep in a wedding weekend, even obliged to prepare the bridal bedchamber.

But she'd accepted his job offer, knowing weddings were an important feature of his resort.

What's more, Hayley had witnessed her employer destroying any chance of a blissful union between him and Leila. In fact, he suspected Leila was probably trying to decide which lucky man she'd get to escort her to whatever glitzy party topped her agenda that weekend. News would soon get around that the heiress was back on the singles scene.

Craig expected some of Leila's circle to laugh at him for breaking things off. He fully expected to receive a frosty phone call from Mr Borthwick — or even a tearful one from Leila's mum, though he'd often thought that particular lady felt her future son-in-law wasn't quite the one she'd wish for.

But it didn't matter now the whole

engagement bubble had burst and he saw it for what it was. A charade. Yet, somewhere back in that heady first emotional tsunami, he'd felt strongly enough about the golden girl to propose.

She had kept him dangling in an emotional limbo before accepting, and now, he wondered whether Leila had been stringing along some other fellow while deciding which was her better option.

He shouldn't be so cynical. Nor should he eavesdrop, even if he found the temptation to learn more about Hayley too powerful to resist.

Craig pretended to examine an open file, while straining not to miss one scrap of conversation from across the way.

'Unlikely people? You mean like me and Jake?' Maria sounded amused.

'No, why should I think that?'

'Because I'm a few years older than he is?'

'Well, Maria, you could've fooled me.

I thought Jake was a few years older than you.'

'Thanks,' Maria said. 'I think!'

Hayley chuckled.

'Trust me to put my foot in it.'

'Not at all. And speaking of what some folk might consider an unlikely relationship, dare I ask how things are going with you and Rusty?'

Craig frowned.

'What relationship?'

Craig relaxed a little.

'Kitchen gossip says Chef reckons you're the sweetest item on his menu.'

Craig held his breath, hardly noticing how his hands were making fists. How his fingernails pierced his palms.

'What rubbish! I teased Rusty about putting chopsticks on the table and he played along.'

'You say that, but after you guys shared a kiss, some people started laying odds as to when you'll have your first date.'

Craig concentrated on taking several very deep breaths. He couldn't bear the thought of hearing Hayley's reaction, yet he didn't want to miss it.

It wasn't his concern whether his employees chose to socialise, OK, frolic, with one another or not, provided they did their jobs well. But he longed to hear her deny the idea of Rusty becoming her Mr Right.

The sudden ringing of the office phone brought him to his senses. Craig sat back in his chair and when his office extension rang, he picked up immediately.

'Mr Borthwick wishes to speak to you, Craig. He's ringing from Melbourne.'

'I wonder what took him so long? OK, put him through, please, Hayley.'

* * *

A huge silver moon lit Hayley's way as she hurried towards the honeymoon cottage. Once inside, she flicked a light switch and headed for the bedroom. Her job was to switch on a lamp for soft

120

background light and scatter fresh rose petals on the pillows.

She was about to leave, but jumped as the door burst open.

'Everything all right? I came to check whether I needed to light the wood burner, but it feels fine in here, don't you think?'

'Yes, I don't think they'll need the fire,' Hayley said. 'We'd better make ourselves scarce. Maria let me know Jake was about to drive them here.'

'Good team work.' Craig followed her down the path. 'The guests will party beyond midnight but you're off duty now. Mind if I walk you back?'

'There's really no need.'

'I asked you a question.'

'You're welcome to keep me company.'

They walked in silence for a while before he spoke.

'I think everything went brilliantly today. I'm proud of all my team, including you, Hayley.'

'Thanks, yes, it's been a good day. I

only played a small part though.'

'Everyone's role counts. And I do feel I might have shown a little more sensitivity towards your feelings.'

She frowned up at the moon. No help there then.

'I'm not sure what you mean.'

'I get the feeling you might find other people's weddings touch a nerve. Maybe you've gone through the emotional mill in the past? And I played the double whammy by breaking off my engagement, didn't I? Maybe that brought back bad memories.' He hesitated. 'I'm making a pig's ear of this.'

She stopped walking.

'I haven't a clue what you're talking about.'

He stopped, too, his face looking troubled in the silvery moonlight.

'You don't have to pretend. I may be your brash Aussie boss, but if you want to let rip about some pesky guy back home, feel free!'

Hayley considered. Craig seemed to

have invented a complicated love life for her. Maria was taking an interest in what she obviously considered as Hayley's loveless state. Rusty may or may not have boasted about his chances with the British girl. Perhaps it was time to set the record straight.

'OK, it's been a hectic few days and I'd appreciate a chat.'

'I'd take you back to my cottage, except I don't want to risk your reputation. There are still plenty of people about and if we're seen, well, need I say more?'

'According to Maria, some of your staff are laying odds on me and your chef getting together so, if anyone sees me with you, at least it'll give them something new to chat about.'

He cleared his throat.

'Fair enough. No-one would take any notice if I invited a staff member into my office for a confidential chat, now would they?'

She didn't answer. Surely he realised an invitation to join him in his cabin at this time of evening was something very different from a discussion at his office?

In His Arms

Of course he knew a shortcut, away from the main track, through woodland. When leafy tree branches crowded out moonlight, Craig guided her by the elbow, unlocked the back door and guided her inside.

'Welcome to my place.' He switched on the light and began drawing curtains.

'How come you have two outside doors?' She shivered and rubbed her bare arms.

'An estate worker would have lived here once, so it's a renovated cottage, not new like most others. I skulked round the back, hoping only a stray kangaroo or two will have spotted us.'

'So the roos come out at night?'

'They do. I think you'll find they're crepuscular.'

She wrinkled her nose.

'They like the twilight. Now, how about something to drink? I could use some supper, too.'

She laughed.

'I enjoyed my meal earlier, but a snack sounds great.'

'I'm afraid there's only bread, cheese and salad.'

'A feast!'

'Why don't you forage in the fridge while I light the wood burner? You're obviously feeling chilly.'

If he only knew his power to send shivers down her spine!

'It's been so warm today, I left my jacket in the office.'

'We do experience sudden temperature changes in these parts. Here, allow me.'

Before she could protest, he shrugged off his jacket and draped it round her shoulders. Her head swam as warmth caressed her arms and shoulders.

Hayley closed her eyes, trying to

compose herself. Trying not to reveal how much she was falling in love with Craig Maxwell.

'How about you pour us some wine? A drop of red will warm you up. Top shelf of the dresser.'

Hayley appreciated having something to concentrate on, while Craig coaxed the flickering flames into action.

She carried his glass over and he smiled into her eyes.

'Take a sip.'

Hayley felt the mellow wine caress the inside of her mouth, velvety and hinting of berry fruits and sunshine.

'Good? This one's a favourite of mine — not too spicy, I hope?'

'It's delicious, thanks.' Concentrate, Hayley, she told herself. 'I couldn't find the butter. Have you run out?'

'No, I hate it straight from the fridge. I keep some in the cupboard.'

She must have opened the wrong door, because Craig was beside her in moments.

'Almost the right place.' His breath

tickled her cheek as he reached for the dish.

Hayley took out bottled salad dressing, a jar of chutney and a bag of salad. She'd already set cheese and bread on the scrubbed pine table.

'Let's load up our plates and picnic by the fire,' Craig suggested.

By now, the logs were radiating welcome warmth. Hayley helped herself to food and Craig carried her glass to the coffee table before the settee and settled into the armchair opposite.

'Here's to many more successful functions.' He raised his glass.

'I'll drink to that.'

'I notice forward bookings are up on last year's.'

'I'm pleased for you.' She put down her glass. 'I won't beat around the bush, Craig. I'm happy here, but I wish people wouldn't try to push me into dating. You, of all people, know our time off is precious. I'm doing my best to learn my job, not — not trying to impress a man just for the sake of getting a date!'

Craig buttered a chunk of bread.

'Maybe people just want you to enjoy yourself?'

'Maybe, but I realise I shouldn't have teased Rusty yesterday. It wasn't very professional and I can assure you it won't happen again. You must've wondered why on earth you ever brought me here.'

'I've never, ever, regretted my decision,' he said softly. For moments they held one another's gaze. 'Anyway, no harm done,' he said, more briskly this time.

'If you've heard Rusty has his eye on me, it's only kitchen gossip, as I told Maria when she mentioned something.'

'Ah, so Maria's involving herself in your love life, is she?'

'Oh, Craig, I have no love life. That can only happen if and when the right man feels like I do and — and, whoever I might decide is the right man is hardly likely to be interested in me!'

'I understand the gossip makes you

cross, Hayley, but no-one means any harm. They've taken you to their hearts, that's for sure.

'But I agree you shouldn't be in a hurry. The right guy's out there somewhere, maybe feeling exactly like you do, and when the time's right, it'll happen.'

She couldn't fathom the wistful expression on his face and looked away, fearing he'd see the tenderness in her eyes, an emotion inspired by his lovely, wise comment.

He rose, holding his empty plate and glass.

'Can I get you something else to eat?'

'No, thanks. I really should go now. It's late.'

'So soon? It's not like you have to work tomorrow! If I remember rightly, you're down for a day off.' He topped up her glass while she was still trying to think up a suitable response.

'One more drink will help you sleep. I can smuggle you into my car and drive you back so you're tucked up well before midnight.'

'All right. Could I say something else?'

'Feel free.'

'I hope I'm not speaking out of turn here, I'm sorry you had to break off your engagement but I think you must have given your decision a huge amount of thought.'

'Some folk will consider me foolish not to hang around and help Leila empty her father's money bags.'

'I already told you I admired you for not letting her wealth influence your decision. But it's not about money, is it? It's obvious how much this place means to you. The lifestyle . . . being able to saddle up Flame when you want. All the things you couldn't do in the city.' She hesitated.

'A lot of people depend on you for their livelihood. If you sold this place, who knows what a new owner might do with it?'

Craig's silence made Hayley wish she hadn't commented. She excused herself and headed for the bathroom.

Left alone, Craig stared into the fire. Hayley sent mixed signals. She was obviously supportive and not afraid to speak her mind, though he'd hate to incur her displeasure. He grinned. Poor Rusty! He didn't think much of his chances with the lovely British girl.

This thought caused him some heart-searching. If Hayley had confessed warm feelings towards the chef, how would he have felt? Craig knew the answer. Right from the first, even before splitting from Leila, he'd detested the idea of Hayley and his chef getting together.

Wasn't it time to admit he wanted Hayley for himself? Dare he trust his instincts? He and Leila were clearly incompatible but he wished he'd had the courage of his convictions sooner rather than later.

'That sky's perfect.' Hayley's voice broke his reverie. 'I've never seen so many stars. You'd never experience that in the city, whether it was Melbourne or London.'

He turned to look at her. He longed to take her in his arms though he couldn't find words to tell her. She walked towards him and Craig got to his feet and pulled her close, firmly but tenderly so she could pull away if she wanted.

His breath caught in his throat as he felt her melt into his arms. Should he ask if he might kiss her? No way. That could break the mood.

Her lips felt soft and yielding beneath his. He felt her kiss him back. Their arms were around each other. Craig's world stood still, though only for moments as he heard a banging on the front door.

Hayley wriggled from his arms and fled to his bedroom, closing the door behind her. He took a deep breath, feeling bereft.

Inside Craig's bedroom, Hayley strained to hear the conversation. Something was definitely wrong. After she heard the front door shut, Craig opened the bedroom door, his expression concerned.

'What's wrong?'

'I can tell Jake's had a hard time, though he played it down. One of the wedding guests had drunk way too much and when a barman suggested he shouldn't have any more, the guest punched him.'

Hayley gasped.

'How awful!'

'Yep. Someone sounded the alarm and the security man stepped in. Maria's putting ice on the victim's chin and the party's breaking up, but I need to get across there.'

He stepped closer.

'Honey, I'm so sorry. I feel embarrassed, but top marks for being so quick-witted. It saved you from being placed in a compromising situation.'

'It's OK. I realise you must go.'

'I think it's the proper thing to do.'

'I'll make myself scarce.'

'Hayley, no! I doubt I'll be long and

it sounds like Jake and Maria have everything under control. Just in case of repercussions, it's important I speak to the barman, especially as he's not one of my permanent staff. I wish you'd wait here for me.'

How could he say such a thing? The evening's enchantment had vanished and, to hang around wasn't her style. No way would she make herself seem so readily available, not even for Craig.

'I don't think that's a good idea.'

She sensed his disappointment but was grateful he didn't argue, even though the urge to be held by Craig and to feel his lips on hers again burned bright as the fire in the stone hearth.

His Worst Fears

'You missed all the drama last night.' Maria looked up as Hayley joined her at the breakfast table.

Hayley frowned.

'Drama? What happened?'

Maria described the incident, almost exactly as Craig had.

'Oh, my goodness.' Hayley needed to summon her acting skills. 'Did everything calm down?'

'Some of the guests were angry that the young man got himself in such a state. Luckily, Jake called Craig and he came across and talked to people while we played soothing music and served coffee and sparkling water. Pity the poor person who had to play nursemaid to one very under-the-weather young man.'

'Thank goodness things didn't get too ugly.'

'Good teamwork saved the day! Now, given half a chance, I'd mug you for that frock you're wearing! Such a gorgeous floral print.'

'I thought I'd give it an airing as I'm off duty.'

'It wouldn't be connected with Rusty having a day off too, I suppose?'

'No, it would not!'

'You look like you didn't get much sleep last night. Are you feeling OK?'

Hayley reached for the marmalade.

'I'm fine. It's probably because yesterday was so busy. I might walk into town this morning and browse the shops.'

'Coming from a different country, you'll probably find them interesting. Try the café. You can't miss the owner's magenta hair, though it might even be green or blue since last time I saw her!'

'I expect I'll call in for a cuppa. Now, are you sure I can't help at all? With Craig out and me not around, do you have enough staff?'

'Craig's driving guests to the station.

He'll be back soon. Kitchen's covered and the wedding party decided to organise their own barbecue this evening, remember? So you go and enjoy yourself though I'm afraid you won't find much doing in our little town.'

'The walk will do me good and if the bookshop's open, I'll be well away.'

'It's not too dull for you here, is it, Hayley? You seem to enjoy your job but it's hardly Melbourne when it comes to having fun in your spare time.'

'I'd have tried to find a job there if I was that keen to stay in the city but I'd have needed somewhere to live. This job suits me well.'

'Good to hear.' Maria drained her cup. 'I'd best get on, but you have a good day and if you're too tired to walk back, give me a bell and I'll find someone to rescue you.'

'I'll try not to bother you, but thanks, Maria.'

Hayley finished her breakfast, deep in thought. After that special moment last night, how would she and Craig behave towards one another now? Would he ask her for a date? Could they recreate the magical interlude they enjoyed in the firelight the previous evening?

But her boss's recently ended relationship sent the word 'rebound' ricocheting around her head. Life must go on as if their mutual flare of attraction never happened. It was far safer that way.

* * *

Hayley had strolled from the resort into town and explored the main street. Now she wanted to check out the second hand bookstore.

The air inside cooled her face and bare arms. There was no sign of anyone and she closed the door and stood, admiring the book-crammed shelves. But a selection of old postcards caught her eye so she began riffling through, intrigued by those depicting former eras, with street scenes and formal family portraits attracting her most.

Did all those people earn their living from cattle or sheep or growing crops? There was a picture of a teacher, tall, hair scraped into a bun, standing by pupils who probably wished they were kicking a ball.

Then, in a heart-stopping moment, she spotted a postcard featuring young men standing on or around a tractor. It might have been taken at some kind of agricultural show, but what fascinated Hayley was the man in the driver's seat. He was a dead ringer for Craig Maxwell.

She picked up the card, peered closely at it then decided she must buy it. That could be one of Craig's forebears in the scene. But what if she handed over the card and it meant nothing to him?

'Are you a collector?'

She was locking gazes with a man who might have belonged in a smart city gallery rather than a country bookstore.

'No, I'm just interested in bygone times. These postcards are pieces of history.'

The man nodded.

'Yes, I often wonder about the folk the camera captured.' He looked at the card she held. 'Are you interested in ancient farm machinery?'

Hayley laughed.

'No way. To be honest, the gentleman in the driving seat looks very much like my boss, but I could be mistaken.'

'You're British, aren't you?'

'I am. I'm working at the resort.'

'Thought as much. So you're Hayley?'

'Yes.' She raised her eyebrows.

'Clara at the café told me Craig Maxwell had a new employee. I'm Don.' He nodded towards the card. 'May I take a look?'

'Of course.' Hayley handed it over.

'I haven't seen this picture before as my daughter sorted this batch, but I agree about the resemblance.' He turned the card over to inspect the postmark. 'I wouldn't mind betting we're looking at Craig's great-great grandpa here.'

'So do you think he'd like to know about this — in case it really is who you think it is?'

Don shrugged.

'Why don't you give it to him? With my compliments.'

She felt relieved when the bookstore owner moved off to answer the phone. Of course, everyone would know everyone else in this small town. Don's gesture was kind, though she suddenly felt shy about giving the postcard to Craig. She chose a few cards for herself before selecting a couple of paperbacks.

'Thank you for your custom.' Don placed her purchases in a brown paper bag. 'Let me know if we were right about that Craig Maxwell lookalike.'

'I will.'

She walked into what felt like an oven after the cool bookstore so headed for the café. After a drink and a snack, she'd visit the wash-room and apply more sun cream. She was almost there when she heard someone call her name.

'Hi, Hayley! Two minds with but a single thought.'

'So is this how you usually spend your day off, Rusty?'

'Nope, I sometimes visit my folks or my married sister who's about two hours' drive away. It's not a very exciting life, is it?'

'I imagine it must suit you or else you wouldn't be here.'

He laughed, a loud, splendid laugh. Gestured towards the café.

'How about we go inside? Unless you're meeting someone . . . '

'I'm on my own.'

'Then, allow me.' Rusty moved towards the door. 'After you, ma'am.'

At first Craig thought he was imagining things. That his yearning for Hayley, to hear her husky voice speaking in that lovely English accent, to see her sweet smile, was projecting her image on to any young woman who fitted the bill.

He could see her standing on the

pavement, wearing a floaty dress and looking as though she'd stepped straight from a watercolour of an English rose-garden.

Here was the girl who occupied his thoughts much more than was good for him. He was about to pull over, ask if Hayley wanted a lift back — wanted to be driven somewhere else — wanted to talk about the night before.

But someone was holding open the café door. Misty Mountain's chef had his gaze fixed on her and no way could Craig butt in. Despite her protests, she must have a date. With so much on his mind, Craig had completely forgotten Rusty also had a day off.

So, for them to spend some free time together was understandable. Except, Craig couldn't bear to think of Hayley enjoying anything more significant than a cool drink and a doughnut with Rusty.

He continued driving towards his beloved resort, leaving behind the girl with whom he knew he'd fallen in love. Craig felt nothing but black despair.

Too Many Broken Hearts

Hayley knew the chef could work magic with food but she hadn't realised how much he enjoyed sending himself up.

'You have a fabulous laugh,' Rusty said after finishing yet another rib-tickling kitchen anecdote.

'Really? I hadn't thought about it.' She looked round. 'Here comes our brunch. You must enjoy having someone else cooking for you.'

They waited while plates of poached eggs and sour-dough toast were placed before them. Hayley could see what Maria meant about the café owner. She wore a purple and pink stripy top over scarlet cut-offs and she'd tied up her bright pink hair in a rainbow scarf.

'Enjoy.' Clara gave Rusty a meaningful look before moving off.

'Thanks, babe.' He leaned towards Hayley. 'Why were you gabbling like that? After you changed the subject, I mean.'

Hayley picked up the pepper mill.

'Was I? I thought we were still discussing food.'

'I was paying you a compliment.'

'Actually, I think Clara has a soft spot for you.'

'Yeah, well, we're good mates.' He cut into his toast. 'She's a great girl, even if you need your shades on to look at her, but there's nothing between us.'

'I think she'd like to be something more than your good mate.'

'No way! I wouldn't mind if that comment applied to you, though.' He shot her a mischievous look.

'I'm not girlfriend material.'

'What's that supposed to mean?'

This was awful.

'It's the truth. I've had boyfriends in the past, one who was very important to me, but coming over here was meant to be a complete break — a chance to consider my options. About my career, I mean.'

'A bit drastic, isn't it? Flying almost seventeen thousand kilometres to have a think!'

'Any idea what that is in miles?'

He put down his fork and took out his phone. After a few moments he looked up.

'Give or take, it's about ten and a half thousand.'

'Yikes! I tried not to think about the distance while I was in mid-air.'

'Don't blame you. But about this career thing — how long are you planning on staying out here?'

'I'll need to return to the UK before my visa expires, so I can stay until the post holder returns.'

'And have you reached any conclusions — apart from being sweet on the boss?'

Hayley's fork clattered to her plate. Hastily, she grabbed it and wiped her fingers with her paper napkin.

'Come on . . . you know it's true.'

'Funny how everyone seems to have an opinion about who I may or may not have my eye on. It's ridiculous!'

'You look even more beautiful when you're angry.' Rusty was demolishing his plateful. 'I wonder if I can persuade you to come out with me tonight.'

Hayley reached for her glass of orange juice.

'I thought I'd made my feelings clear.'

'But you're in danger of not making the most of life, girl.'

'Because I don't want to go out with you?'

'Because you're mooning like a lonesome heifer over a guy with too many emotional scars to risk getting involved with another girl, especially one who'll run off and leave him on his own again.'

'Is that so?' It was horrible, hearing her inner fears voiced.

'Too right it is. The poor guy's suffering. Everyone knows the heiress was taking Craig for a ride but he has to work that out for himself before he can move on.'

'So you're a relationship counsellor as well as a chef?'

Rusty rolled his eyes.

'Leave the boss to sort himself out and have some fun with me. I'm single, not looking for a wife, and I have no hang-ups. Well, none I'd admit to.'

Despite herself, Hayley laughed.

'You don't believe in wrapping things up, that's for sure. But why do you want to date me when there are plenty of girls around here who'd go out with you?'

'Kitchen gossip!' He picked up his cup. 'Yeah, there's one or two I wouldn't mind seeing again but that way lies danger, English girl.'

'What kind of danger?'

'I don't want to commit myself to a relationship. My contract here ends next March and I might go travelling again. I don't plan on leaving any broken hearts behind.'

'You reckon you're that much of a catch?'

He chuckled.

'I enjoy female company and I need to remember, if I take up with one of these local ladies again — and I know I'm jumping to conclusions — she might read more into it than I bargained for.

'Getting away from Misty Mountain now and then is good for me. Good for all of us, I'd say. So, next time we have the same day off, maybe you and me could drive to the coast, have dinner and, well, maybe stay over somewhere and come back early next morning ready for duty, no worries.'

Hayley stared back at him. He was an attractive young man, but although she couldn't deny feeling flattered, someone else was tugging at her heartstrings.

'I guess my chat-up line's fallen on stony ground. I must be losing my touch.' Rusty pulled a woeful face.

'It's more like I am.'

'Got it bad, have we?'

Hayley couldn't speak.

'OK, don't answer that. I can tell how things are by your expression.'

'Is it that obvious?'

'Yeah, but your secret's safe with me.'

She managed a wobbly smile.

'Maria thinks you and I should get together.'

'She's one bright lady. Got a lot of respect for her, but I have for you as well. If the boss is who you want, I wish you luck, but like I said, if you do get together, don't let him break your heart.'

'I doubt that'll happen, but thanks for the advice.'

'How about an ice-cream now?'

'You go ahead. And finish telling me about that summer job you had in London.'

'Only if you let me take your photo — even better a selfie with you, so I can post it on line and make my mates jealous.'

'Oh, you do talk rubbish.' She relented.

'I suppose, if any of my friends back home see it, it can't do my street cred any harm.'

Before they left, Rusty offered her a lift back.

'Don't forget staff can use the swimming pool afternoons,' he said, steering his car along the resort's driveway. 'I might take a dip later.'

'I won't forget, thanks. But just now, I feel like I could sleep for a week.'

'So, take a nap and recharge your batteries.'

He pulled up near the staff cabins and hopped out to open the passenger door.

'Thanks for looking after me.' Hayley stood on tiptoe to kiss his cheek.

A movement caught her eye. Her boss was walking in the direction of the stables. Hayley noticed the grim expression on Craig's face as he so obviously tried to avoid making eye contact and she needed all her willpower not to run after him and explain she wasn't flirting with Rusty. Something told her this wasn't the right time.

★　★　★

'Enjoy your day?' Georgie glanced up as Hayley walked into reception later.

'Very much, thanks.'

'Maria will be here soon to relieve me. If you fancy company, I can take my meal break with you.'

'Lovely, I'll wait for you, then. What's on the menu?'

'Thai red curried fish with rice and veggies. Or chicken salad.'

'Fish sounds good. Shall I order for you, too?'

'Make it two fish, please.'

Hayley went through to the dining-room. She didn't particularly want to discuss her day out, didn't want to keep protesting about herself and Rusty. She enjoyed his company but that was all. She ordered the food, sat down at a table and pulled a paperback from her handbag.

Georgie appeared the moment the book's hero arrived on the page.

'Hey,' she said. 'I've just checked my phone and guess what I saw?'

'Me, maybe?'

'You bet! Are you and Rusty an item now?'

'Not unless you know something I don't.'

'He refers to you as his lovely mate from England but that might be a smokescreen.'

'We bumped into one another and had brunch in the café.'

'Pity.'

'It was delicious — no need for pity!'

'I meant it's a shame you're not dating. You need something to brighten up your life.'

'No I don't!' Hayley glanced up at the student helper. 'Thanks very much. That looks scrumptious.'

Georgie waited until the young man left.

'We're all longing to know what brought you halfway across the planet. Rusty's convinced there must be a guy behind it.'

'Look, I was made redundant and decided it was time I did something entirely different. I'm still in touch with a friend who emigrated with her parents and she invited me to stay with her in Melbourne. I saw this job advertised and for some reason, the boss offered me the position.'

'Bad luck about the redundancy but good on you for finding a job quickly. Mmm, this fish is yummy. Rusty's made sure his assistant knows her stuff.'

Hayley was about to change the subject when Georgie beat her to it.

'You're working at the race course tomorrow, aren't you?'

'Yes, but I don't know why Maria chose me.'

'Maybe she didn't. Maybe the boss decided.'

Hayley froze.

'No pressure then. Is this some kind of test?'

'No way. It's a compliment to be chosen actually. You'll be looking after the people in the Gold marquee, which means most of the wedding party plus other hotel guests.

'Maria will brief you in the morning

but it should be fun. You get to take the canapés round and fetch drinks for guests. It's a bit like being hostess at your own party.'

Georgie forked up another chunk of fish but not before dropping a virtual bombshell.

'The boss will be there too. I think the groom's father is an old friend of Craig's dad so he wants to keep a close eye on things.' She paused. 'I expect he'll drive you.'

*   *   *

Hayley regretted taking a nap earlier because here she was, still wakeful at midnight and facing a busy day with a difference.

Craig had been absent from the dining-room, so when they met again, their stolen kiss would be that little bit less recent. Maybe he'd already banished it from his thoughts. Pity she couldn't do the same.

Punching her pillow yet again,

dangerous thoughts still haunted her. Tantalising images refused to disappear. How she felt when Craig first put his arms around her and his lips sought hers was still vivid. She knew she must forget what happened but how could she bear to lose something so precious?

Was this how love felt? She'd often wondered. Dreamed about there being a man out there somewhere, waiting for her. Deep down, Hayley knew she'd been lacking someone special in her life and now she'd found him. Except she wavered between wanting Craig to know how she felt and not wishing to begin something destined to end in heartbreak.

This was no way to prepare for a busy day. Craig Maxwell was first and foremost her boss, not her potential boyfriend. She might secretly hope for more, but wasn't that pointless?

Maybe she should stop daydreaming and start counting sheep. Or kangaroos.

Caught Unawares!

Next morning, when Hayley met Craig, he was polite. Businesslike. Nothing about his demeanour hinted at anything unusual as they walked towards his vehicle. Hayley clambered into the passenger seat before Craig could suggest she drove. To her dismay, her tummy turned somersaults whenever she glanced at his profile or caught a drift of sandalwood cologne.

Her boss took a call on his mobile phone, arranging to meet with someone later. She sat beside him, her hair scooped up and away from her face, her fingernails manicured to perfection, her make up discreet and her scent, a gift from Jacqui, wafted peonies and roses.

The sun shone but the weather forecast warned of storms later. Hayley shifted her position as Craig started the engine.

'I hope you enjoyed your day off.'

Maybe she imagined the slight edge to his voice?

'Yes, thanks. I bumped into Rusty and we had a bite to eat.'

'Right.'

'He's very fond of Clara at the café. I expect you know her?'

'Yes.'

He was starting to remind her of her mum's TV favourite, the stern Doc Martin. Hayley gazed through her window, wishing she could break this barrier, but what could she say? Did he wish he didn't have to drive her, making polite conversation?

After a while, she could see the signs and colourful pennants announcing they were almost at the racecourse.

'I guess Maria's briefed you?'

'She has, thanks.'

'She and Jake will follow on. By the way, you look very smart, Hayley. I'm proud to have you on my staff.'

Hot tears stung her eyelids. She found this remark oddly hurtful, but why couldn't she accept that was all she was to him? OK. She'd work her socks off today. Charm all his guests. And if that didn't please her infuriating boss, she'd resign and return to Melbourne. Or anywhere she could find another job.

Craig stopped at a barrier where an official fixed a badge on the windscreen before waving them through. They'd arrived early enough to park alongside their marquee and unload everything.

'Don't try lifting anything,' he warned.

'There are a couple of lads to do that. You might like to familiarise yourself with the layout of the stalls, wash-rooms, etc, so you have all the answers if our guests ask for directions.'

'All right.' Hayley hitched her shoulder bag into place.

'Remember to note where we are so you can find your way back.'

Did he really think she was that dim? He must have read her mind because his lips twitched and he hesitated as if about to speak. But he turned away to unload a floral arrangement. So Hayley began her walkabout.

The gold marquee stood in the middle of the first row of stands and facilities. Others, offering less luxurious options, were either side. Some race-goers gambled on good weather so they could picnic on the grass and use the coffee stalls and bars dotted around.

Maria greeted her when she returned.

'Craig told me he'd sent you off.'

'I expect he'll be surprised to see me back so soon.'

'Sorry?'

'He seemed to think I might get lost.'

'Are you OK, Hayley? Just that you seem a bit . . . '

'I'm fine. What happens now?' Hayley glared at Craig's back.

Maria blinked hard.

'The public are allowed entrance at eleven so we've time to relax a while. Weather should be all right for a few hours, but we could cop some squalls later.'

'It's as bad as being in the UK, then.'

'Surely not!'

Time sped from then on. Hayley couldn't believe the variety and colour of the outfits she saw as race-goers streamed into the grounds, heading for the marquees and best vantage points.

She hadn't expected to see so many young people, couples, small and large groups, sometimes all female, with the girls vying to turn heads. Hayley spotted halter necks, cold shoulder sleeves, strapless dresses and skirts her grandma would describe as pelmets. The thought tickled her.

'Private joke or can anyone join in?' Maria asked.

'I was imagining what my gran would say about some of the fashions.'

'Or mine, bless her.'

'There must be every possible shade of the rainbow out there.'

'And the fascinators! There's a sea of feathers, satin ribbons and felt flowers.'

'Don't forget the sparkles,' Hayley said.

Maria nudged her elbow, seeing the

162

first guests filter into the open-fronted marquee.

'Here we go.'

Craig arrived.

'Maria and Hayley, I'd like to introduce you both to the groom's father. You probably know he's an old friend of my dad's.'

They followed their boss to the far side of the marquee. Most of the wedding party staying at Misty Mountain were present and Hayley found several recognised her and greeted her by name.

Soon she was busy welcoming, shifting seats to accommodate groups of friends or couples on their own and generally making herself useful.

Craig was doing likewise. No way was he taking it easy with the guests. She tried not to get too close but sometimes felt his gaze follow her or caught his eye as she collected drinks or took round another tray of spicy chicken pieces or veggie samosas.

She found herself alongside Maria as

they took a short break to watch the jockeys hurtle past, their gaudy silks rivalling the ladies' dresses.

'I think everyone's having a great time but I've a feeling the weather's beginning to play up.' Maria looked up at the sky.

It was almost three o'clock when Hayley walked back from the wash-room and the first spots of rain made her hurry. Thunder rumbled in the distance. Sheet lightning swiftly followed. She'd hardly reached the marquee when the steadily falling rain became a downpour.

The next race was delayed to allow people to find shelter and, looking round, Hayley noticed the wife of Craig's dad's old friend wasn't in her seat. Hayley made her way across.

'Excuse me, Mr Denman, but I'm wondering whether your wife's been caught out by the rainstorm.'

'I think she must have, my dear,' he replied. 'I've been keeping my eye open for her. Hopefully she's sheltering in the ladies' room.'

'I've just got back from the nearest one. Does she have her mobile phone with her?'

'She hates the things. I keep telling her she needs to get into the twenty-first century but she won't listen.'

'Would you like me to see if she's marooned in the ladies' room?'

'You can't do that, Hayley. You'll get soaked to the skin!'

'Craig brought golfing umbrellas. I'll take one and see if I can find your wife.'

She hurried past Craig, who was talking on his phone, picked up an umbrella and unfurled it before setting off. Already it was slippery underfoot but she wore black leather flatties and got along at a brisk pace, to find several women were sheltering, some looking enviously at Hayley beneath her Mary Poppins brolly.

She folded that down but held tight to it and, muttering apologies, squeezed her way inside. Sure enough, Mrs Denman stood at the back of the little crowd and Hayley saw her face brighten when she spotted her.

'I noticed you were missing so had a word with your husband. We can wait for a while and hope the rain stops, or we can walk back. There's plenty of room for both of us under here.'

'To tell you the truth, I'm frozen, my dear. Shall we make a run for it?'

Outside again, Hayley opened the umbrella and Mrs Denman grabbed her arm as they dodged muddy patches. They were halfway between wash-room and marquee when Hayley felt Mrs Denman's grip on her arm tighten.

She exclaimed as her foot slid on a muddy patch and, despite Hayley's efforts to stay upright, the two of them collapsed in a heap while the open brolly bounced on the soggy turf.

Before Hayley could do anything, two young men ran forward and helped her and Mrs Denman to their feet.

'Thanks, guys.' Hayley grabbed the umbrella one of her knights in shining armour had rescued. 'Mrs Denman, are you OK?'

'I'm not hurt, my dear. I'm so sorry I pulled you over — we must look like two scarecrows.'

'Never mind that!' a male voice said. 'So long as you're both all right.'

Hayley cringed. What a mess she must look. More importantly, would her boss think she'd used bad judgement, going off like that?

'Poor Hayley — I pulled her over with me when I slipped, Craig. She was kind enough to come and find me. I'm so very sorry.'

'Let's get you back.'

'But I can't go in there, looking like this!'

'No, we must spare you that. I'll drive you back to your cottage. You take my arm and shelter under the umbrella. I doubt you'll manage to pull me over.' He turned to Hayley. 'You follow in my footsteps, Hayley. You're coming, too.'

'But . . . '

He silenced her with a glance and she

followed behind until Craig stopped beside their marquee.

'The organisers have cancelled the last race, for safety reasons. We'll leave via the service gate and I can return for any equipment Jake and Maria can't fit in their vehicles.'

'But I left my bag under the bar.'

'I'll fetch it when I go and tell Mr Denman I'm kidnapping his wife.' He handed the umbrella to Mrs Denman and turned to Hayley. 'Here's the car key. I'll be with you in a minute.'

Hayley watched him disappear inside.

'Let's keep walking,' she said. 'Just think of that lovely, hot shower waiting for you back at your cottage.'

* * *

Before they set off, Craig covered the passenger seats with old rugs salvaged from the car boot. Hayley stayed in the vehicle while he escorted Mrs Denman to her cottage, using a master key to unlock the door. He turned to Hayley as he got back behind the wheel.

'There's nothing wrong with her that can't be put right by a hot shower. I've told her we'll send her dress to the dry cleaners.'

'It's lucky you provide us with spare uniforms.' Hayley leaned forward as he reversed his car. 'I can easily walk from here, Craig. I can't get any muddier than I am and you'll want to get back.'

'Jake and Maria will supervise the lads. I don't want you to catch cold, Hayley, plus I'd like to be sure you're still in one piece. I saw what happened back there. Mrs Denman landed on top of you so you came off worse than she did.'

'My hip's a little sore, that's all.' She winced as she sat back.

'Then you need a hot bath.'

'A hot shower will do.'

'Rubbish.' He swung the vehicle in the opposite direction.

'Where are we going?'

'My cottage.'

'In broad daylight? What'll people think?'

'People can think what they like. I want you in a hot tub.'

Hayley's jaw dropped. He caught her eye in his rear view mirror and laughed.

'For goodness' sake! I mean, we need to run a hot bath for you to take a soak while I make a pot of strong tea, by which time, hopefully you'll feel a whole lot better.'

'Is there any point in arguing?'

'None whatsoever.'

Neither of them spoke until Craig pulled up.

'I doubt anyone's strolling out here on such a dismal afternoon. Not that it matters, though I'll have to ring Georgie and ask her to fetch you some clothes. I can hardly drop you off wearing nothing but a towelling robe.'

'This is awful. I'm causing so much trouble.'

'Come on, out you get. It wasn't your fault. You were using your initiative, carrying out a good deed, so please stop protesting.' He grinned. 'Would you prefer me to fetch your clothes?'

It was a relief to laugh.

'Maybe Georgie's my best bet after all.'

Once they were inside, he switched on a small fan heater.

'This'll do till I light a proper fire. Meantime I'll fetch a gown and you can get undressed here and come through when you're ready.' He was back in moments, carrying a fluffy white bathrobe and a pair of the lightweight mules the resort provided for guests.

Hayley stared at him.

'A lot has happened since the first time you brought me a gown.'

He stared back. Cleared his throat.

'Yes, well . . . I'd better run that tub.'

Hayley felt bemused. He was being so kind, so considerate, but didn't his businesslike manner prove he'd put on his hotel proprietor mask? She told herself he'd have been equally helpful towards any other staff member.

She was folding her damp, mud-streaked uniform when he called.

'Ready then, Hayley? Have a good wallow. I put some pine bath salts in, to help soothe any bruises.'

'You're very thoughtful.' Hayley put down her washing bundle.

'I'll make some tea. Take your time and I'll knock when it's poured.'

A while later, soothed by the warm, pine-scented water and hearing occasional chinking of crockery from beyond the wall, she wondered if Craig did need to return to the racecourse. She really should get a move on.

She gazed around. Her own cabin possessed only the basics but apart from this big tub, her boss's accommodation looked similar to hers. She wondered how the heiress enjoyed staying here without the kind of luxuries she was used to. Too much state of the art equipment wouldn't fit the country holiday image Misty Mountain aimed for.

Hayley moved her fingers and gently

probed her left hip. She pressed a little harder, but it seemed to have suffered no ill effects. Maybe all it had needed was a good hot soak, as her boss prescribed.

She wondered how long she'd been in the tub and lifted her head to hear if he was moving round. Nothing. She'd better get out. She was, after all, still officially on duty though she'd lost track of time.

That thought kick-started her into action. Getting to her feet, she realised Craig must have pushed the bath stool and towel away from the tub while the water ran. Hayley, when removing the robe, had flung it on top of the towel without thinking.

She reached over to let out the water. Both chain and plug were made of heavy copper. As she let the chain swing free, the metal plug clanked against the bath and the water gurgled and slurped noisily on its way down the waste pipe. Hayley stepped on to the bathmat. The door opened. And in walked Craig, carrying her mug of tea.

'Why didn't you knock? You said you'd knock!' she yelled, using both hands to shield herself.

'I did knock! You couldn't have heard me. I'm — oh, heck, I've spilled your tea now. I'll have to put the mug down.'

'Never mind that. Throw me a towel!'

'It's all right. I wasn't looking because I was trying not to spill the tea.'

'Craig, for pity's sake . . . '

'Sorry. Ouch! Let me put this tea down before I scald the other hand.'

'Run the cold water tap on it! But only after you pass the towel.'

Getting to Know You

The moment he heard her place her empty mug on the counter, he left his bedroom, wearing jeans and polo shirt.

'I thought maybe you'd gone to the office,' she said.

'Everything's under control. More to the point, how's your hip? I can drive you to the hospital if necessary.'

'Thanks, but there's absolutely no need. I must go back to work.'

He glared.

'Please tell me you're not serious?'

'I certainly am.'

'Hayley, stop fretting about me walking in on you. I'll apologise again if it helps.'

'Please don't change the subject, boss. I can't have put in my hours today.'

'Just relax and please stop calling me boss when we're alone.' He moved a little closer. 'It's been a stressful day. Why don't you stay for a glass of wine and I'll fetch us some supper?'

'I don't think that's a very good idea, do you?'

'Yes, Hayley, I most certainly do. That's why I suggested it.'

'Is Mrs Denman all right?'

'She hit a lucky streak at the races so she's ordered champagne for their family party. Mrs D is fine and singing your praises. I just spoke to her on her husband's phone.'

'Any news on the wedding guests . . . and that poor barman?'

'Fortunately he's made of stern stuff and doesn't intend taking things further. He's been given some cash and the guest in question has apologised. Now, is there anything else bothering you?'

He watched her smile and needed to clench his fists behind his back to stop himself from taking her in his arms.

'Hayley, you have to listen. I wish I

176

could stop thinking about you because I get the impression you'd prefer that to happen. How could you even contemplate going back to work?'

'I'm not a quitter, Craig. Also, I happen to enjoy my job.'

'I'm aware that's true on both counts. But today you've worked hard, charmed our guests, been at everyone's beck and call, braved the elements and ended up dragged down in the mud like a rugby player!'

She narrowed her eyes.

'You Aussies and your rugby. You're worse than the Welsh. And you've even stolen their weather!'

He grinned.

'Having spent time in Britain, I can't argue with that. But, we're avoiding a proper discussion. And, looking at you, it's like I can't think straight.'

'You've had a stressful time lately.'

'You can say that again.'

'And you're probably experiencing the rebound thing.'

'Why do you have to be so darned

sensible? So annoyingly calm and English?'

'Probably because I am English.'

He spread his hands, palms upward, in exasperation.

'Don't you trust me to know my own feelings?'

'I . . . I think I should go now, Craig. In fact, I know I should.'

'Then why don't you do just that? Go on, Hayley! If you truly feel nothing at all for me, if you tell me that kiss we shared the other night meant nothing to you, then take my car and drive yourself back to your cabin.'

He dug in his jeans pocket, took out his key and threw it to her, eyes blazing.

'Go on!'

She caught the key deftly, balancing it in the palm of her hand. Panic flashed through her body and for moments she forgot to breathe. Rain. Slippery roads. What if . . . ?

But something else prevented her from walking away. He caught his breath as she moved closer.

'You're so beautiful. So graceful,' he whispered.

'Even in my jeans and sweatshirt? I must remember to thank Georgie for delivering them. Did she give you an odd look?'

'Nope. Every one of my fabulously loyal staff is a five-star employee.'

They stood a heartbeat away from each other.

'Well?' he challenged. 'What are you waiting for?'

'I'm waiting for your phone to ring. Or for someone to bang on the door, or — or . . .'

'Or what?'

'Or for you to kiss me again.'

His heart was pounding faster now.

'In that case, you need to know I'm not interested in a one night stand.'

'Great, that makes two of us.'

'Nor am I even looking for a brief fling.'

She hesitated.

'You're thinking about your visa

restrictions, aren't you, my practical Hayley?'

'It's important, Craig. You know I don't have the right to an open-ended stay.'

He pulled her to him, tucked a strand of her hair behind one ear and kissed the tip of her nose.

'Problems arise. Problems are solved. Now, do you think we could stop talking and get on with that kiss?'

He didn't wait for an answer.

★　★　★

Was it hours or minutes they'd been entwined on the big leather couch? Talking. Laughing. Catching up with one another's lives before they met. They gazed into the flames of the log fire, each admitting they couldn't bear to break the spell by thinking about food, but before he drove her back, Craig insisted on making omelettes for their supper.

After he shut the doors on the

washing up he joined her again on the couch.

'So where do we go from here?'

'I go back to my place and see you at work tomorrow.'

'We go on as normal?'

'What else did you have in mind?'

He took her hands in his and kissed her fingers.

'May I say something?'

'Go ahead,' he said.

'I love you, Craig. You don't have to answer but it's important you know I've loved you for a while now, despite torturing myself with questions.'

'Is this to do with my broken engagement? Believe me, darling girl, what I felt for Leila is nothing compared to my feelings for you. If I'd had the sense, I should have broken things off months ago, before you even arrived.'

'It's still early days. We both need time to get used to being around each other.'

'I don't disagree, but because of our

working hours it's impossible for us to date. And don't think you're the only one giving serious thought to our situation because I've been doing that too. While I wasn't torturing myself, wondering if you and Rusty were an item and becoming very grumpy.'

'I've no idea what made you think that. He's a friend and even if I was keen, which I absolutely am not, he's only interested in fun and games.'

'So you two did discuss the matter?' Craig stroked her cheek. 'It's OK, I shan't bark at you.'

'I'm sorry if it bothered you.' She leaned forward and nuzzled his neck.

'Don't be sorry. Nothing else in the world matters when we're together.' He hesitated. 'Why don't we be totally honest about our feelings and announce to everyone that you're moving in?'

'Craig, you know we can't live together!'

'Why not? It is the twenty-first century, you know.'

'I'd never look Maria in the face!

Anyway, it's far too soon.' She plucked up courage. 'I'm also fighting some personal demons.'

He sat up.

'About your feelings for me?'

'No! Why would I say I loved you if I wasn't sure? But you see how that proves my point? We need time to get to know one another before making any decisions.'

He rose, went over to the fireplace, threw on another log and stood, watching orange sparks fly up the chimney. She waited, wondering whether she'd upset him.

He turned to face her.

'I understand where you're coming from. I may not like what you say but it makes sense. Can we agree on two very important things before I drive you back?'

'It depends what they are.'

'This getting to know one another better. What kind of time limit will you set?'

Hayley stood up.

'How can I possibly answer that? You're right when you say we can't go out together except maybe now and then. But even working together — we'll find out things about each other and in a way, that'll be better than going out for a meal, surrounded by strangers.'

'Fat chance of that happening! Unless I change Rusty's free day so I can take the same day off as you.'

'You're incorrigible.'

'Also determined.'

'I won't accept any special favours, Craig. No extra time off so I can spend it with you, tempting as it might be.'

'I wouldn't dream of offering it, Hayley. But I do have something in mind and I hope you'll approve. Now, what are those demons you mentioned?'

★ ★ ★

Hayley let herself into her cabin, glancing over her shoulder as Craig reversed his vehicle and parked it outside the main building. She knew he'd be touching base with his restaurant manager. Georgie would be already off duty. As if Hayley had conjured her up, her colleague appeared, walking from the direction of the hotel.

'I just saw Craig so I thought I might find you here. Are you all right, Hayles? No problems, I hope.'

'None at all.' How lovely to hear the affectionate nickname! 'I'm sorry you had to bring my stuff across. Craig was paranoid about me having a hot bath after I complained my hip was a bit sore after I fell. I think he was afraid I'd be laid up or carted off to hospital.'

'No worries. I gather you came a nasty cropper.'

'No harm done — except to my pride and my uniform.' She gestured to the carrier bag in her hand. 'The staff washing machine's going to be working overtime.'

'You do have a clean outfit for tomorrow?'

'Yes, thank goodness. I just want to go to bed and not dream about rain and mud. I wasn't expecting Aussie weather to be quite so similar to ours back home!'

Georgie chuckled.

'Can't help you there. But I shan't delay you any longer. Just wanted to check all was well.'

Hayley let herself into her room. Georgie must have drawn the curtains earlier. Had she also drawn her own conclusions as to why Hayley needed to remain in the boss's cottage for so long? But whatever plan Craig was cooking up, it better not be anything to cause gossip. She'd need a very cool head from now on.

At least she'd confessed to him the reason for avoiding getting behind the wheel. He hadn't reprimanded her for not mentioning it at her interview and told her they'd discuss it in the morning.

With or Without You

'I wish you'd told me before.' Craig rose as she came into his office next morning.

'I was afraid it might affect my chances.'

'What d'you take me for? These things take time and it must have been terrifying, seeing a pedestrian suddenly in your path.'

'Even at twenty miles an hour Dan couldn't avoid . . . '

'I know.' Craig's voice was gentle. 'At least the man who ran out couldn't have known much about it.'

'No, thank goodness, but Dan was torn apart. And I was always going to be a reminder.'

'I hope you feel better now you've told me?'

She nodded.

'Much better. I still feel ashamed

about my lack of confidence, though.'

'No need. Maria did mention something to me and I remembered how you crawled along that first time. I put it down to you not having driven an automatic before.'

'I'll tell Maria.'

'Tell it like it is and don't try to rush things.'

'You'd think I'd be fine driving on the estate but that panicky feeling still gets hold of me.'

'You disguised it well that time you drove me. Maybe you should try sitting in a vehicle, listening to relaxing music.'

'And have everyone making comments about the batty Brit?'

'We'll find a way. Now, how would you feel if I asked you to take your next two days off together? And soon.'

'Did I hear you right?'

'I need to visit Melbourne to sort out some personal matters.'

'And you need me to cover some of Maria's hours? That's fine.'

He shook his head.

'Thanks, but Georgie's applied for any overtime going. I'm happy for her to cover for Maria, who may need to take on some of my duties in my absence. Hayley, what I'm trying to say is, would you like a lift to Melbourne so you can catch up with your friend?'

'And get to spend time alone with you?' She pretended to think. 'I suppose I might be able to put up with it.'

'Well, that's a relief.'

She saw the sparkle in his eyes. Her heart skipped a beat. That sparkle was what had been missing, making her wonder what troubled him.

'I'd like us to get away soon, so once I confirm my appointments, you can ring Jacqui.' His brow furrowed. 'I also need to visit my parents and explain my decision to end my engagement. We'll need to spend two nights away.'

Hayley hesitated.

'You know Jacqui's boyfriend shares her apartment? I slept on the living-room couch before, but I'll have to check whether he's OK with me visiting.'

'I kind of hoped you'd stay with me. Doesn't that make sense? You'll be right next door to Jacqui.'

She raised her finger to her lips.

'Craig, we can't discuss this now. Guests are arriving.'

'All right, but please give it thought. After all, no-one here's going to know where you stay, unless you tell them.'

She longed to agree, but her determination not to hurry things prevented her.

'Let's speak later, then.' He followed her to the foyer.

Hayley heard him call the guests by name and watched him take suitcases from the elderly gentleman. Craig's love of his business and determination to make it prosper shone in everything he did. It was a trait she admired.

But he had emotional baggage as well as business affairs to deal with in the city and she needed to discover how deeply he felt about her before allowing their relationship to go further.

Was she being naïve to expect a man of Craig's age and sophistication to accept such a situation indefinitely?

★ ★ ★

Hayley didn't see him again until supper when she found him seated at the long table, talking to Jake. She took her meal over, returning their greetings, but deliberately sitting beside a waitress, one whose mum had waved goodbye to her family in Scotland and accompanied her new husband to Melbourne 30 years before.

Hayley, always fascinated by people and their stories, loved hearing how her colleagues had come to work at Misty Mountain.

'So, still enjoying being here?' Debbie smiled up at her.

'Yes, thanks, Debs.' Hayley settled herself.

'I heard about the boss rescuing you.'

'Uhuh, more importantly, he rescued one of the guests.'

'He's gorgeous — yet not arrogant with it.' Debbie put down her fork. 'Hayley, d'you mind if I ask you something personal?'

Hayley's heart plummeted. What was coming now?

'It's about Rusty. He's asked me on a date.' Debbie lowered her voice. 'I've always liked him but I didn't think I stood a chance. He used to have a girlfriend in town, then you arrived . . . but this morning he asked me out for a meal, when we can arrange a suitable time, of course. I said yes, but I don't want to upset you.'

Hayley could have hugged her.

'Of course I'm not upset. I think Rusty's a great guy. We went for brunch together the other day but we're friends and nothing more. I'm so pleased for you both.'

'I couldn't see the point of keeping him waiting but now I'm wondering whether I sounded too eager.'

'I'm sure he wouldn't think that. Deep down, men are often as shy as we are and he's probably thanking his lucky stars you said yes.'

'Let's hope you're right.' Debbie glanced down the table. 'Oho, boss alert! Poor Craig. People say he was wise to end his engagement but I guess he must be lonely.'

Hayley looked up. Craig was walking towards them, coffee cup in hand.

'Good evening, Craig, this goulash is delicious. Did you have it?' Debbie asked.

'Yep, always enjoy Rusty's goulash. Do you two ladies mind if I park here a moment?' He pulled out the chair next to her.

'I don't want to seem rude but, unless you need to talk to me, boss, I must get back to work.'

'Of course. Far be it from me to incur the wrath of our maitre d'!'

'I'll let you know how things go, shall I?' Debbie smiled at Hayley.

But her comment wasn't lost on

Craig. He waited until she left the room.

'Everything's all right with her, I hope?'

'Never better. Don't you dare tell anyone, but Debbie and Rusty are going on a date.'

'I thought my chef looked pleased with himself earlier. You must know how relieved I am, especially now you and I have, well . . . you know what I'm trying to say.' He looked around to make sure no-one else was within earshot.

'Of course. And it's nice news about Debs and Rusty, except . . . ' Hayley hesitated.

'Except what?'

'When people were gossiping about him and me, it was a blessing in disguise.'

'Aha . . . and since your, er, mud bath, and my clumsy attempts at playing Sir Galahad, your supposed romance with my chef's no longer hot gossip. Is that it?'

'Try not to look so intense! Maybe we should pretend to have an argument.'

'No way will I pretend to argue with you and for goodness' sake stop murmuring like that — I'm sure people will start wondering what we're cooking up.' He groaned.

'I'm hopeless at this sort of thing. I wanted to tell you I've arranged appointments for Thursday so we need to set off Wednesday after your shift ends. Did you contact Jacqui?'

'Her phone was switched off so I e-mailed. I'll let you know what she says when she gets back to me. How about Maria?'

'No worries. She thinks it's a great idea for you to catch up with your old friend.'

He checked his watch.

'I need to ring my folks and find what time would suit them for me to call.'

'I'll go and sit with Georgie. She's on her own over there. I'll give you a call later. Is that all right?'

'Excellent.' With that, he walked away. He was right. Each of them seemed uncertain how to act in public. Maybe time together would help them as Craig hoped.

But after Hayley returned to the office to check her e-mails, she found nothing from her friend, so sent Craig a quick text.

He rang at once.

'She could have forgotten to charge her phone or maybe she's tied up with work stuff. All kinds of things could explain it.'

'I'll try again tomorrow.'

'But you'll still join me, even if you can't contact her?'

'I — I'm not sure, Craig. It makes my coming with you kind of pointless, don't you think?'

'Pointless! The point is we have a rare chance to be together, Hayley. And you'll enjoy shopping or sightseeing while I'm seeing people. Just being alone together is what I long for.'

She closed her eyes briefly.

'You make it sound very tempting.'

'Good. Darling Hayley, this is a chance to have fun together, don't you see?'

'I just need a little longer, please. I'd like to be sure it's OK to stay with Jacqui.'

'My apartment's larger than hers. I have a guest bedroom and you'll be quite safe there. Maybe I need to get a lock fixed on the door?' He sounded hurt.

'Please don't think I'm trying to be difficult. But it was you who suggested I might like to catch up with Jacqui. Am I to tell her all I want is a bed for a couple of nights because I'll either be out sightseeing, or with you? That sounds like taking advantage of her hospitality, don't you think?'

'I'm not sure what to think. I shall leave for Melbourne at five o'clock Thursday afternoon. With or without you.'

★   ★   ★

Craig spent a restless night. He hadn't meant to speak so sharply. What if Hayley thought him arrogant and bossy? But if they were to deepen their relationship, they needed to spend precious time together.

He'd remained in his last relationship far too long. For months, he'd been a peacekeeper — picking his way through a minefield even, given Leila's reputation as a diva. Now he couldn't understand why he waited so long.

Hayley entered his life when he'd still been engaged. He'd felt an instant attraction, but maybe because this bothered him, he probably came across as a little offhand. Noticing her name among the applicants for the vacant position struck him as something of a coincidence.

He still believed he'd made the right choice. But Hayley had changed status from employee to the woman he knew he wanted to spend his life with. Now he wondered if the intensity of his feelings was scaring her.

How could she possibly understand that no way were his feelings for her anything to do with being on the rebound.

Craig threw back the duvet and padded over to the window. Although moonlight silvered the landscape, he saw no sign of wildlife though there was certain to be plenty around. Sometimes you found it impossible to see something even though it might be right under your nose.

Now it dawned upon him how he'd been rushing Hayley. She'd scarcely had time to find her feet in a new country, when he whisked her away to work for him, hundreds of kilometres from Melbourne where her only friend over here lived.

He headed to the kitchen for a drink of water. Hayley could call the shots from now on. Unless she didn't want to risk giving her heart to a battle-scarred man like him . . .

Fighting Her Demons

It was almost lunchtime, with Craig still avoiding her. Now she had to speak to him. Afternoons were usually quiet and she could leave his door ajar, in case anyone entered reception. He opened it within moments of her knock and beckoned her inside.

'Take a seat, Hayley.' He returned to his chair. 'Before you say anything, I must apologise for the way I spoke to you yesterday evening. I was out of order and I'm sorry.'

'I'm partly to blame so please don't beat yourself up. I've heard from Jacqui at last. She and her boyfriend are in Hong Kong. The company he works for want him to relocate and Jacqui asked her boss if she could take a few days' leave and go with him, to see how she feels about moving there.'

'Fair enough.' Craig twirled a pen between his fingers. 'Even if you can't stay at her flat, the offer of my guest room stands.'

'I think it's time I was totally honest.'

'I'm listening.'

'I want to come with you, but I don't want to risk rushing into things.'

'Things?'

'You know exactly what I mean.'

'I love seeing you blush.'

Hayley shook her head at him.

'Sorry.'

'Maria thinks I'm visiting my friend, so how can I face her after we get back and she asks how I got on? I can't tell lies, Craig. The only way out is for me to stay at a hotel. You must know of one nearby?'

'There's one that friends of mine sometimes use so I'll book you in for two nights. OK?'

She beamed.

'Perfect. I can pay for my own accommodation, of course. I'll tell Maria Jacqui's gone away but I've decided to go anyway, so I can see more of the city.'

'Just leave the hotel to me.' He leaned forward, taking her hands in his. 'Knowing you want to be with me as much as I want to be with you makes me very happy, Hayley.'

The reception bell pinged. Craig had closed his door without her noticing.

'I have to go.'

He stood up.

'And I need to drive to my parents' house. If I'm seeing them in Melbourne, I daren't admit I haven't checked on their new home lately. I'll be back in an hour or so.'

Hayley dealt with a guest's query about trains. She felt as though a ton weight was lifted from her shoulders. If she and Craig were both determined to put their relationship on a firm footing, that must be a very positive thing.

★ ★ ★

As dinnertime approached, Hayley took a call from one of the rooms in the main building.

'Good evening, Mrs Henderson. It's Hayley. What can I do for you?'

'I'm sorry to trouble you, my dear, but my husband went out walking an hour ago and he hasn't returned. He said he only wanted a short stroll and I can't help worrying.'

'Could he have decided to go into town? If so, he's probably on his way back.'

'I doubt he'd walk that far.'

'I'll see if I can find someone to look for him.' Hayley did her best to reassure her.

'That's so kind. I'm not keen on driving nowadays.'

Hayley knew the feeling.

'I'll get back to you after I've spoken to my manager.'

She knew Maria was on lifeguard duty, so hurried to the swimming pool where Maria was perched in her watchtower. Hayley explained the problem.

Maria looked at the swimmers, frolicking in the water.

'I daren't leave these guys. Go and have a word with the boss.'

'He's gone to check progress on his parents' new home so he'll be at least an hour.'

'I'd ask Jake but he's fixing a dripping tap in a cottage where we have guests checking in later.'

'It's down to me, then.'

Maria shook her head.

'Hayley, you've confided your problem and I don't think you should force yourself into driving. It's pointless you going on foot, and I hate to say it, but if Mr Henderson's in difficulty, he'll need medical attention and how can we call an ambulance if we don't have his location?' She looked at Hayley. 'You're ignoring me, aren't you?'

★ ★ ★

Hayley approached the estate car as if going into a lion's cage, desperately hoping the missing guest would stroll down the track before she could start the engine. Beside her trotted Mrs Henderson.

'This is so kind of you, dear.'

'Not at all.' Hayley prayed she wouldn't hyperventilate. 'It's part of my job. Anyway, I'm sure your husband can't be far away.' She hesitated before opening the passenger door. 'You're quite certain he didn't take his phone?'

'Positive. It's still in our room.'

She helped Mrs Henderson settle into the passenger seat. OK, Hayley. You can do this. You can. Don't forget to rest your left foot. Remember you don't need it.

She turned the ignition key. The engine sputtered into life. One deep breath, then another and the vehicle was moving forward.

'What was your husband wearing?' Hayley's lips felt like they did when the dentist gave an injection.

'Denim jeans and checked shirt. He took his panama hat.'

'Very wise.'

'Do you have a cold, Hayley? You sound a little croaky.'

Nerves could do that to people.

'I'm fine. Could you keep a watch on your side, while I keep an eye to the right?'

They were nearing the main entrance. Which way?

'Shall I drive towards town?' She swallowed involuntarily. 'Or the highway?'

'Probably not the highway.'

Hayley turned left, offering a silent prayer of thanks for being able to drive on the same side of the road as back home. She was almost at the town boundary sign when her passenger pointed and gave a shout.

'I see him! He's just there, beside the road.'

Hayley indicated and pulled over.

'Stay here while I talk to him.'

She jumped out and jogged back towards the man slumped on the grassy verge.

'Mr Henderson?' No reply. Hayley bent down. 'Can you hear me?'

Nothing. Gently she touched his cheek and caught her breath when his head flopped backwards. There was no-one in sight. No passing traffic either. She felt for a pulse. Panicked when she found nothing. Heaved a relieved sigh when she did. There was no sign of any bleeding or bruising.

Hayley managed to get him into the recovery position.

'Stay with us, sir! I'll be back in a moment.'

She turned to find Mrs Henderson dropping to her knees beside her husband.

'Tell me he's alive! Oh, Hayley, what's wrong with him?'

'He's breathing but we must get him to hospital. Keep talking to him while I move the car.'

She hurried back to her vehicle and reversed so she was closer to the casualty. She switched off the ignition and hopped out again. So far so good

— but things were about to become more challenging.

'Mrs Henderson, do you think you can help me get him into the back seat?'

'Of course I will. And do call me Jane, but can't you phone for help?'

'No signal. And I'd rather drive your husband straight to hospital than have to stop to try ringing. But, please own up if you have back problems. I daren't let you hurt yourself.'

'I'm a tough old bird, my dear. I'm up for this!'

Hayley grinned.

'Fantastic. Tell me when you're ready and I'll lift him into a sitting position. We'll try to get him on the back seat then.'

'Ready when you are.'

Hayley thanked her lucky stars Mr Henderson was of slim build. It wasn't difficult to get him sitting up though she didn't know whether to be pleased or worried to hear him groan.

'We're lifting you now, sir.'

Hayley knew this next manoeuvre would prove tricky. Had she not been driving this great brute of a car, with wide-opening doors, she'd have been in danger of hurting the elderly man. His head was still slumped on his chest and she muttered a heartfelt thank you when she managed to get his top half on to the back seat.

'I need to get round the other side and ease him along while you look after his legs. Now, Jane. On my count of three . . . '

*   *   *

At the hospital, Hayley was as relieved as her companion was, to learn this collapse was probably due to heat exhaustion though Mr Henderson would undergo tests.

She turned to his wife.

'Shall I fetch some tea?'

Jane Henderson didn't answer but Hayley had suspected reaction might set in once they reached the safe haven of hospital. She put her arms around her.

'Let it all out, Jane. You've been so brave.'

The woman gulped and took the handful of tissues Hayley offered.

'So have you, my dear. You had to talk yourself into driving, didn't you?'

'Was it that obvious? I, um, once had a horrible experience as a passenger and ever since, I've been a bit of a wimp, I'm afraid.'

'Well, you certainly weren't today. I'm so grateful.'

'Before I fetch our tea, I'll give Misty Mountain a ring. Just in case they decide to send out a search party.'

Such bliss to find a signal! Hayley stood outside in the evening sunshine and rang reception. Maria answered quickly and Hayley updated her then heard Maria give a potted version to someone close by.

'Craig's here beside me, Hayley. He rang in to check if everything was OK and now he's back and wants a word.'

Hayley bit her lip. Tears were close and as soon as she heard his voice, she struggled to find even one word of greeting.

'I'm coming to the hospital. I'll get someone to ride with me and bring Mrs Henderson back. I'll drive us home in the estate car. Hayley? Do you understand what I'm saying?'

'I'm . . . yes . . . so sorry to be a nuisance.'

'Get someone to fetch you a cup of tea, my darling girl. I'm on my way.'

He rang off. Hayley couldn't stop trembling. Her legs felt like jelly but she'd done it. She'd driven on the highway and kept her passengers and herself safe.

As to what Maria must have thought, hearing Craig call Hayley his darling girl, she couldn't imagine.

A Good Omen?

'Do you realise we haven't stopped talking for the last hour and a half?'

'Are you saying I'm stopping you from concentrating?'

Craig shot her a wicked grin.

'You've been affecting my concentration ever since the night we met. As an engaged man, I wouldn't have tried to see you again, but you made enough of an impression to shock me into thinking seriously about my life. My relationship with Leila was over and something had to be done. She's probably still angry but I expect she's already found my replacement.'

Hayley hesitated.

'Craig, have you considered how people might say the same of you? It's a good reason for us to keep a low profile, don't you think?'

'You're right. I know what I feel for you isn't a flash in the pan. But it's way too soon to declare myself. I wouldn't want there to be even one shred of gossip or malicious remark about us. Does that make sense?'

'Yes, it does.'

'I want to show you off, but you're quite right about not going to places where I might bump into certain people. And we'll find a way to handle things when we get back, too. I know you understand how not just my business but my heart is in Misty Mountain — even more so since you arrived.'

'That's a lovely thing to say. The worst thing is worrying whether anyone suspects anything's happening between us.'

'I suspect something rather wonderful is happening between us.' He spoke quietly and the warmth in his voice brought tears of happiness to Hayley's eyes.

'Here's a hotel where we can get a

good meal coming up on the left.' Craig began to slow down.

★   ★   ★

'That was the best dessert! Cherries, chocolate and vanilla ice cream — yum.'

'The cheese selection was much more interesting. There are a couple I should mention to Rusty when we get back,' Craig said.

'Wearing your business hat again?'

He chuckled.

'Sorry.'

'I'm only teasing. It was a delicious dinner. And now we know we both enjoy reading, watching movies and . . . '

Craig laughed.

'And neither of our mothers ever missed an episode of 'Neighbours'!'

'You prefer hotter, spicier food than I do.'

'Not a problem, as long as you don't make me eat desserts. Though I make an exception for Rusty's lemon tart.' Craig checked his watch. 'I'll settle up and see you outside.'

She strolled out of the restaurant. It was a cool evening, a little overcast but the sun hadn't yet set. Craig joined her and put his arm around her waist as they walked to his car. When they were both settled, he leaned in, giving her a long, tender kiss.

'Mmm . . . ' He sat up straight, buckled his seat belt and put his key in the ignition. Nothing.

'That's odd,' he muttered.

She needed to drag herself back from the place his kiss took her.

The engine fired at the second try. But as he reversed, Craig muttered again and this time it was a mild but heartfelt curse.

'What's wrong?'

'The red warning light's come on. I'll drive slowly out of the car park but if it doesn't turn itself off, I won't chance our luck. There are too many kilometres between here and the next town.'

Hayley waited while Craig consulted the hotel manager. When he came over to her, he explained the position at once.

'The good news is the manager knows a local car mechanic and he's ringing to ask if he can help.' Craig ran his hand through his hair. 'Fact is, Hayley, I've very stupidly let my AAA membership lapse, so we're not in the best of positions. I'm so very sorry.'

Hayley shrugged.

'You've had loads on your mind. You should let me make diary notes for that kind of thing.'

'Do you want to fetch a book or play some music while we wait?'

'Let's see how long the man takes.' Hayley wandered over to a stand stuffed with tourist information leaflets. 'We have a better selection than this.'

Craig joined her.

'Now who's wearing her business hat? But thanks for offering to organise me. That would be a great help.'

She nudged him.

'The manager's back.'

It seemed the motor mechanic had been on his way home but wasn't far away. When he arrived, Craig walked him to the vehicle and Hayley followed them a few minutes later.

Watching the two of them talking, she wasn't surprised when Craig turned to her.

'This guy can sort it out but he'll need to collect a part so won't be back until tomorrow morning bright and early. We'll have to stay overnight, provided they have rooms.'

'Oh, that's such a shame. It could've been worse, though.'

'I love the way you see the bright side, Hayley. Tell you what, we might as well go straight in and ask for accommodation. I can collect our bags once we know where we are.'

Inside, a young woman stepped up to deal with them, listening as Craig explained their plight.

'That's bad luck,' she said. 'However,

we do have one double-bedded cabin available.'

'Just the one?' Craig bit his lip. 'We really need separate rooms.'

Hayley felt, despite the situation, an uncontrollable urge to giggle.

'Are you sure there's nothing else?'

The receptionist shook her head.

'I'm sorry, sir. Would you like to take the room?'

'Unless you can recommend somewhere within walking distance, I'd better say yes. I can sleep in the back of the car,' he told Hayley.

Aware of the receptionist's curious gaze, Hayley stood aside as Craig registered.

'I'll bring your bag in now,' he said.

They walked in silence to his car.

'Just your bag?' he said. 'You won't need this jacket, will you?'

'No, thanks. Hey, I hate to think of you sleeping in the car.'

'I'll be fine. I'll lock myself in.'

She sighed.

'It seems ridiculous. You're being

218

very gallant, but your legs are too long for you to have a comfortable night on the back seat.'

'I'll survive.'

'But you're the driver. Unless, maybe I could . . . '

'Darling, you're not insured for my car.'

She felt a rush of relief.

'I just don't want you getting stressed.'

'Nor me you!' He grinned. 'Now, let's take your bag to the room and go and have a drink.'

He locked the car.

'Come on. The room's down at the other end of the row.'

Inside the cabin, he looked around.

'This looks OK, don't you think?' He made a face. 'Except for those yellow curtains.'

'They're a bit flimsy, I suppose, but the bed looks fine.' She sat down on it then stretched out. 'It's very comfortable.' She sat up. 'You need to fetch your bag, too.'

'I do not.'

'Really? So how will you brush your teeth? And you'll be desperate for a shower.'

'I can use the hotel wash-room.'

'It doesn't seem fair for me to have this room all to myself.'

'You're the one determined to take things slowly. I'm not too sure I can handle being your room mate.'

'What if I say I trust you?'

He kissed her before releasing her.

'OK, you win. I'll fetch my bag but we'll talk things through.'

★　★　★

While Craig ordered drinks, Hayley chose a table far from the big TV set. Opening her handbag, she took out the envelope containing the postcard she'd kept secret from him. When he returned with a glass in each hand, she smiled up at him.

'I have something for you.'

He put down the drinks and sat beside her.

'You've been buying postcards?'

'Yes, but not today. I was browsing a collection of very old ones at Don's shop a while back and came across one you might find interesting.'

He glanced at the card.

'Old timers, having a chat?'

'Look more closely.'

He peered at the image then gave a soft whistle.

'I recognise the tractor driver. Did Don point him out to you?'

'I noticed a resemblance between the two of you. Don came to see if I needed help and he agreed it could be one of your forebears. So I was right?'

Craig didn't take his eyes off the postcard.

'You surely were. Wow, Hayley, thank you so much for spotting this. May I buy it from you?'

She chuckled.

'No, silly. Don said he wanted you to have it with his compliments. Apparently, your mother used to use the bookstore but not recently.'

'She'll be in and out of there again once they settle in the new house. But it's my father who'll be most thrilled with this find. George Maxwell would've been born in the late 1860s. Well, what d'you know!'

Craig continued examining the picture.

'Was this picture taken on the Misty Mountain estate?' Hayley asked.

'I'd say so. The land was farmed back in those days. My father's told me bits and pieces of family history over the years but I don't want to bore you.'

She shook her head.

'I won't be bored. This wine's delicious, by the way.'

'Good.' He took a sip of cold beer.

'Well, it's my great-grandad George who suffered the most, it seems. He was probably paying his way by farming the land, selling stock and working with one of his brothers plus his two sons and a daughter who was a good poultry keeper. But after the New York Wall Street Crash, everything changed.'

'I never thought about Australia suffering. My nana used to talk about the Depression and how the majority of people got by any way they could.'

'George was into his sixties when everything went pear-shaped so it must have been hard for him, wondering what kind of business his son and his son's son — my dad — would be left with.' Craig stared into space.

'I hope,' she said gently, 'I haven't stirred up unhappy memories.'

He reached for her hand.

'Not at all. We have very few family photos from around that time.'

'I imagine they were too busy earning a living to dress up and have their pictures taken.'

'Probably.' Craig's expression became dreamy. 'The farm survived, picked up again and by the time World War II began, my grandfather was busier than ever. But maybe that land wasn't destined to be farmed long-term because, in the 1970s, my dad decided to sell some and use the money raised to build a hotel on the remainder.'

'He had an eye to the future.'

'Yep. The business has changed over the years. Dad hadn't drawn up plans for the cottages but when I returned from boarding school for the holidays when I was about fourteen, I got quite a surprise.'

'And that's when you began taking an interest?'

'I couldn't wait to leave school. My mother suggested I should travel first and work in hotels in the UK.' He lifted Hayley's hand to his lips and kissed it. 'Here I am, rambling on about the Maxwell clan when I'm sitting next to the most beautiful girl I've ever met.'

'I love hearing about the past. George Maxwell was the founder of a dynasty. He established an enterprise on the Maxwell estate, even if agriculture gave way to the leisure industry. That was a wonderful achievement.'

'Thanks for understanding.'

There was no need for Craig to tell her how Leila never got her head round his love for Misty Mountain. And Hayley knew if things worked out for the two of them, she'd do her utmost to support him and ensure business thrived.

For one brief moment a picture of a small boy with Craig's dark hair and brown eyes flashed into her mind's eye, making her gasp with surprise.

'What's wrong?'

'Absolutely nothing.' It was her turn to squeeze his hand. 'Weird things happen sometimes, that's all. I like to think my coming across that old postcard might be a good omen.'

Another Think Coming

At first she couldn't understand why buttery sunlight was shining through the slats of an unfamiliar blind. Of course, she was in a motel midway between Misty Mountain and Melbourne. But where was Craig and why hadn't he woken her?

She sat up, straining her ears. Yes, there were sounds of him moving around. She got out of bed and padded over to the tea making equipment. Gingerly, she touched a finger to the kettle. How had he managed to make a brew without waking her?

She scuttled back to bed as the bathroom door opened.

'G'day, sleepy-head!' He was dressed for business.

'Hi, how did you sleep?' She stretched her arms above her head.

'Surprisingly well, thanks. I suppose

you'd like a cuppa?'

'Are you spoiling me?'

He switched on the kettle.

'Maybe.'

'Do we have time for breakfast?'

He came closer.

'You're only allowed breakfast if I'm allowed a cuddle.'

'I love you, Craig.'

He stood looking down at her, his expression serious.

'And I love you, Hayley. I . . . I find it difficult to tell you how much you mean to me.' He hugged her then broke away. 'I'd better make that tea.' Both of them laughed as his phone beeped. 'Or not!' He checked the message. 'Our good Samaritan has arrived.'

'You go, Craig. I'll come down when I'm dressed.'

'Well, I guess that'd be safer.' His eyes twinkled. 'Now where did I put my shoes?' He picked up his car key and blew her a kiss.

They'd talked for ages last night in the bar and then back in the room after each had undressed in the bathroom. They'd kissed and cuddled. Shared secrets, hopes and dreams — some silly, others poignant. Then Craig took a spare blanket and pillow from inside the wardrobe and settled down on the floor.

Hayley dressed, packed her overnight bag and let herself out of the room. At the other end of the car park Craig stood beside his car while the mechanic worked.

He called to her.

'Our man here thinks we'll be away by eight. So if you want brekkie, you go inside and I'll come and find you.'

'Should we skip it and settle for something when we arrive?'

'Perfect. Leave your bag while you grab a coffee and a piece of fruit at reception. I've settled up so I'll fetch you when we're ready to roll.'

The highway hummed with vehicles, especially on the city outskirts, but they made good time. After he pulled into his underground garage, he cut the engine.

'Let's go to my local café before we do anything else. They make wonderful scrambled eggs and bacon plus a pot of English breakfast tea.'

'My favourite breakfast. What time did you tell the hotel I'd be arriving?'

'Mid-morning, so we're fine.' He hesitated. 'Do you want me to bring your bag now? I'm not sure what you plan to do while I'm seeing people.'

'I'd like to visit the arts centre. They have an exhibition that sounds wonderful.'

'There's also the National Gallery of Victoria. You can walk to both places from here, or take a tram.' He fished in his pocket. 'Take this spare card — there should be plenty of credit on there.'

She nodded.

'I left mine at Jacqui's.'

'Not much call for it at Misty Mountain. How about I drop off your bag after we've eaten and say you'll turn up when you turn up?'

Hayley bit her lip.

'I'm sorry I made a fuss about staying with you. It seems silly now, having shared a room last night.'

He squeezed her hand.

'Your decision, Hayley. I send plenty of business that hotel's way so they're not about to charge for last night. I won't try to influence you one way or the other, darling.'

'I'd like to stay with you, Craig. If you can put up with me.'

* * *

After breakfast, Craig saw her on to a tram.

'Text me later and let me know where you are.'

He walked down the street to wait for a tram that would drop him near his lawyer's office. He still couldn't believe Hayley's changed attitude. It was all about trust, wasn't it?

But, though most of his mates would

jeer if they knew he spent the night on the bedroom floor, while his beautiful companion slept in a king-size bed, he respected her feelings and was pleased with the way things were going.

He wasn't proud of the way he'd acted when unsure whether she wanted to accompany him to Melbourne. But, while certain of his feelings, and hers for him, he still wouldn't push her into making pledges for the future. If she decided to remain in his country, there were ways to help her achieve that.

His mind fast-forwarded to his meeting. He needed to cancel the draft will, written with marriage in mind, and instruct his lawyer to rewrite it.

It seemed depressing to dwell upon what-ifs on such a sunny day but he was a businessman and needed to keep a keen eye on his personal affairs and his resort's future, though he still didn't look forward to visiting his bank.

★ ★ ★

Melbourne provided the perfect opportunity for some retail therapy though it seemed odd seeing festive window displays and browsing Christmas decorations and gifts with the temperature heading for 30 degrees.

Hayley stood inside the main entrance to send a message to Craig.

'Off to Arts Centre. What time should I come back?' She pressed Send. Why hadn't she thought to ask him for a spare key to his apartment? What if Leila still had one? Worse, what if she decided to check up on him? Stop being such a wimp, she told herself.

She was enjoying herself and still had loads to see. She hoped he wasn't having a rough time with his folks, and would hate them to think she was responsible for Craig breaking off with the heiress.

Maybe she should buy some little gift for him, to say thank you for bringing her. She decided to look in the national gallery gift shop where she found a recently published book on the history of Victoria, before heading off to the Kylie Minogue exhibition.

One of the star's videos made her want to dance, while around the room were models wearing Kylie's clothing. Hayley couldn't resist photographing everything, including some wacky, dazzling shoes.

She took a minute to realise she could hear a familiar voice. Her mouth dry from nervousness, Hayley stopped beside a mannequin dressed in gold shorts and sparkly vest, her heart beating faster as the woman on the other side of the display case chatted.

'I'm having a copy made of Kylie's fabulous silver gown, sweetie. My dressmaker's promised it'll be ready for a first fitting soon.'

'Leila, how exciting! So, this is for the December ball?'

'It might be.' The heiress sounded coy.

'And who's your escort? I promise not to say a word.'

'Jim Cranfield's on standby.'

'Wow, Jim's gorgeous, Leila. And far wealthier than Craig.'

'Yes, but I do love a challenge, sweetie. And Jim's hanging on my every word, while Craig — oh, he's just playing hard to get! You know how men can be sometimes. I need a little more time and once that pig-headed fiancé of mine sees sense, there'll be no stopping me. The gala ball will be the icing on the cake once Craig's ring is back on my finger.'

The friend muttered something about money.

'It's pretty important, sweetie. That's why Daddy will make sure I never have to get my hands dirty once I'm married to Craig.'

Hayley's head swam. What was going on here? Surely Craig wasn't deceiving her? Why did Leila still refer to him as her fiancé? She didn't want to believe it, but could it be, having won her confidence, Craig was reeling her in — and if she succumbed, only to find he dropped her, how would she cope with his rejection?

Yet he'd sounded so cut up when he asked her about Rusty. Craig's passionate declaration over being unable to bear it if she cared for his chef had filled her with joy and hope for the future because she cared for Craig in a way she'd never experienced before.

The heiress had dropped her voice. But Hayley didn't care what she said now. The damage was done. Deep down, she'd always suspected she wasn't sophisticated enough for an eligible man like Craig Maxwell.

Maybe, being the businessman he was, he'd opted for financial security and a wife he saw only when she clicked her fingers. Hayley didn't doubt Craig's sincerity over his beloved Misty Mountain but if he thought he could play with her affections while he awaited his password to a fat bank account, he had another think coming.

She slipped quietly away, shielding her face by smoothing her hair, in case the heiress glanced her way.

Hayley smothered a sob as she fled, with no idea where to go. Her overnight case was still in Craig's car. She was alone in a big city. And her only friend in that big city was far from home.

Love is Blind

Craig's meeting at the bank still made him wince. But the time spent with his parents had gone well. He'd felt more relaxed and happy in their company than in a long while.

His mum shed tears when he announced there was no way he and Leila could ever make a go of marriage. He explained how he'd suspected for a while that the whole thing was a mistake, saying he'd honestly given Leila his reasons for ending their engagement. It was only when he moved to his mother's side to comfort her that he realised her tears were tears of joy.

'I need to tell you something else,' he'd said. 'There's someone new in my life. She's a British girl, highly over-qualified for her role at Misty Mountain, but someone who's become far more than an employee. Ma, Pa — I don't expect you to approve and I understand you might worry this is a rebound thing but I love Hayley in a way I never cared for Leila. I'm totally sure of my feelings this time.'

His dad had nodded.

'Your mother and I would never have interfered, son. But neither of us felt Leila was right for you. If you can find happiness with this young woman and if she feels the same, then you have my blessing.'

'And mine too,' his mum had said. 'So, what's your young lady's name?'

'Hayley.'

'Like Hayley Mills?'

'I guess so.'

'Pretty.'

'Sounds as if the two of you'll make a good team to run the business — like your mother and me.' His father shied away from expressing emotion but Craig knew how pleased he was. He also knew he couldn't mention his financial dilemma. Not yet. Not until he'd talked things through with Hayley.

Craig read Hayley's text but decided to surprise her. He loped along the pavement, picturing her sweet face, her long, silky hair, and gorgeous mouth. Was it too soon to ask if they could formalise matters? Did she trust him enough to forget all that stuff about not rushing things?

He bounded up to the main entrance and followed the signs to the exhibition hall. Hayley and her folks were fans of Australia's most famous pop diva. That would go down well with his folks, who'd loved Kylie for ever.

Craig was smiling again, until the girl he loved exploded into his path. She stopped, staring at him as though she didn't recognise him.

'Hayley? Darling, what's happened? Has someone upset you?'

He tried to hug her but she backed away like a fearful puppy. He took a few steps towards her, flinching as she held up her hand in warning.

'Don't come any nearer.' Her voice

sounded strained.

'You're worrying me, Hayley. Please tell me why you're acting this way.'

'Aw, well, what have we here?'

Craig, becoming more apprehensive each moment, turned to face the heiress.

'What's up, honey? Staff problems?' she asked.

He had to stop himself from shaking Leila. Yet Craig's impeccable manners made it difficult for him to snub anyone, even his wealthy ex.

'Hayley and I are leaving. I hope you enjoy the rest of your afternoon.'

Leila clutched his arm. He looked down at her fingernails, shiny violet against his white shirtsleeve. She'd probably arrived fresh from the beauty salon. Craig was vaguely aware of her female companion hovering, no doubt enjoying the show.

'I've nothing more to say to you, Leila.'

Her eyes glittered. She took her hand from his sleeve and slapped his face.

Hard. Craig raised a hand to his cheek.

'Enough.' He turned away. 'Come on, Hayley, let's get out of here.'

But Hayley had gone. Straight away, Craig headed for the door. What had Leila done to upset her? He didn't intend finding out, not when the girl he loved was distressed enough to go walkabout.

His anxiety a tight band around his chest, he stood outside, scanning the patio where tourists and locals relaxed beneath green umbrellas. Hayley would surely go to his apartment building. She had no other option. But being so upset, would she think logically?

Craig spun round as he heard his name called, only to see Leila hurrying towards him.

'Haven't you caused enough upset?' He glared at her, fists balled at his sides.

'OK, OK.' She held up her hands as though in surrender. 'I was wrong, very wrong, to think I could win you back. And I'm sorry I slapped you.'

He nodded curtly.

'You're very cute, Craig, cute as a koala.' He sighed. 'And I adored being on your arm, but you were right all along. You and me, we're chalk and cheese.' She shrugged. 'Back there, I don't know what got into me. Maybe hurt pride — maybe because my friend was boasting about her boyfriend and how she thinks he's about to propose — so, I just let rip.'

'Is that it now?'

'Yes, Craig. I'm sorry your Hayley must've heard what I said just before you arrived.' She didn't look him in the eye.

'And what exactly did you say?'

'About me being able to win you back if I wanted. I, um, might've given the impression we were still engaged.'

'No wonder she left. Leila, I love that girl!'

'Then you'd better run after her.'

Craig beat it.

Leila gazed after him.

'So that's how he acts when he's in love.'

★   ★   ★

Instinct led Hayley back the way she came. She walked blindly, contemplating heading for Jacqui's building and throwing herself upon the concierge's mercy. Even if the night manager wasn't around, she could provide Jacqui's contact details.

What was the time difference between Melbourne and Hong Kong? It didn't matter. If she couldn't contact Jacqui, she could still try that hotel. Also she needed to ring Maria to tell her she couldn't come back. What about her clothes and stuff? At that moment, Hayley really didn't care.

She gasped as she remembered. At her request, Craig held her passport in his office safe.

★   ★   ★

Craig grabbed Hayley's bag from his car. He wished he could have caught her up but she must have flown along the road or maybe flagged down a taxi. He'd walked, scanning the passers-by, until he reached the nearest tram stop.

He let himself into his flat and flung his keys and phone on the coffee table before going over to his neighbour's. Knocked once. Twice. A third time. Nothing.

He returned to his apartment and called up the manager's number. Yes, Ms Collins had explained the misunderstanding causing her friend not to leave permission for Hayley to access the apartment. The situation had been dealt with, by checking with the key holder. Was everything all right?

Craig reassured him. This time he rang Hayley's mobile phone, found she'd switched it off and threw down his phone.

Outside Jacqui's door again, he leaned his head against the wooden panelling and spoke as clearly and loudly as he could.

'Hayley!' Nothing. 'This is ridiculous,' he told the keyhole. 'I know you can hear me. Darling girl, please open the door. I can explain everything. Please believe me. It was a ridiculous wind-up. Leila has confessed she lied when you heard her talking. She didn't even know you were there.'

Nothing.

Craig sighed and went back to his flat. He had to find some way of contacting Hayley. Yes! It was still very hot outside. She might be on the balcony, as this side of the building was in shadow this time of day, providing a welcome oasis. He rushed to unlock his own balcony, leaving the door open behind him.

He leaned around the screen to see if she was out there. No sign. A breeze ruffled his hair, cooling his face.

'Hayley?' He called. 'Please talk to me!'

If she didn't respond, he'd tell the desk he feared the young lady had fainted and her health might be in danger if they didn't get inside.

Sadly for Craig, that mischievous breeze, capable of whipping itself up from nowhere, blew his balcony door shut before he could reach it. In his agitation he'd forgotten to prop it open. His phone lay where he'd left it.

★　★　★

Hayley had caught her tram by a whisker. At her destination, she hurried to the apartment building and found an official she recognised. After giving Jacqui's phone number, and following a quick call, she gained access.

Hayley locked herself in. Should she ring Maria? But why should she be driven away from a job she loved? Nor did she want to disappoint colleagues she'd become fond of. Maybe she should take a train back to the resort tomorrow then give one month's notice. That would give her thinking time.

Someone banged on the apartment door. It must be Craig. Hayley switched off her phone and sat down. Yes, she could hear what he said.

Tears stung her eyes. She wanted to believe him, but why put herself through such anguish? Leila was wealthy. Determined. Accustomed to having her way.

Craig might remember to leave her bag outside the door. Wasn't he known for his gentlemanly behaviour? Now she couldn't hold back her tears.

A Song in Her Heart

Was that someone singing? Hayley couldn't hear properly because the balcony door was shut. It could only be Craig but what was he playing at? Residents might start complaining. Hayley hurried to unlock Jacqui's balcony door and stepped outside.

She wondered if he'd heard her come outside. Despite her mood, Hayley's lips twitched. Craig was singing one of her grandad's favourites 'Do Not Forsake Me, Oh My Darling'.

Unexpectedly, she sneezed. And sneezed again. From the corner of her eye, she noticed a large, white handkerchief waving over the trellis separating the two balconies.

'Bless you.' The handkerchief fluttered down. Hayley picked it up and blew her nose. 'Shall I sing to you again?'

'I question the last song's relevance,' she said icily. 'Surely you're the one that's forsaken me?' She heard a sigh.

'Won't you at least let me explain properly? You heard a conversation in which my former fiancée — I repeat, former fiancée — wasn't telling the truth.'

'How do I know you're telling the truth?'

'Maybe this will help. Today, I visited my lawyer and instructed him to shred the draft will waiting for my status to change from single to married. Because that won't happen now,' he hesitated, 'unless I can convince you how much I love you and want you to be my wife.'

Hayley's knees almost buckled beneath her.

'Another option is for me to call out my mother's mobile number so you can ring her to introduce yourself as the girl I want to marry and tell her you're looking forward to meeting her as soon as possible.'

If she called his mother, wouldn't

that tell him she didn't trust his word? What kind of basis was that for their future?

It was time to follow her instincts. Time to take the initiative.

'I don't think that'll be necessary. I want to look to the future. It's high time we sorted everything out and the best way to do that is to talk face to face. So, shall I come round to you?'

He didn't answer.

'Craig? Did you hear what I said? I'm in dire need of a hug.'

'Me too. Trouble is, I've managed to lock myself out.' He paused. 'Hayley, are you laughing?'

⋆ ⋆ ⋆

'From now on, the only place I want to be imprisoned is right here, with your arms around me.'

'I'm sorry I laughed. And when you began singing 'Send in the Clowns', I just fell about! The receptionist must've thought I was mad when I rang. At least this time it was the night manager again. He should be used to us by now!'

Craig hugged her again.

'Laughter and love and plenty of it, Hayley. That's what I want our life together to hold.'

'Me too.'

'And thank you for your suggestions. Already I feel more hopeful about the business.'

'I'm glad. But please don't say any more about promoting me. I'm happy as things are and, besides, I don't have anywhere near Maria's experience.'

'It's high time I gave our key people the right titles. How about I make Maria our general manager and you our office manager?'

'If anyone deserves that position it's Georgie.'

'So, let's make Georgie our office manager. That still leaves you.'

'I'd love to create a new role. How about making me weddings co-ordinator? I could do more promotion, setting up bridal fairs and so on.' She brushed her fingers across his lips.

'Could you assume that role immediately?'

'Yay.' Hayley snuggled even deeper into his arms. 'Thank you so much, Craig.'

'But I have another position in mind. That is, if you feel you can handle two roles.'

'I'll do my best. What's the other one?'

'Will you be my wife?' He ignored her gasp. 'I realise you have no experience of this role, Ms Collins, but your qualifications are excellent, so I'd appreciate your giving the idea serious consideration.'

She wondered how she could possibly feel any happier than she did at this moment.

'The important thing is we love one another and I want to be your wife.'

'That's just as well.' He paused. 'Where would you like to be married?'

'At Misty Mountain, of course!'

'Not back home?'

'No. My home's with you now and my folks can come out here next year.'

'So, we can set a date?'

'There are weddings booked for every weekend between now and February.'

He whistled.

'You've brought good luck to the resort. Maybe your folks could visit us in March?'

'Brilliant. It needn't be a big wedding.'

'You really think Maria will let us get away with that?'

And when those hands she'd admired the first time she sat beside Craig in his car moved to cup her face tenderly, Hayley knew she truly had come home.

We do hope that you have enjoyed reading this large print book.

Did you know that all of our titles are available for purchase?

We publish a wide range of high quality large print books including:
Romances, Mysteries, Classics
General Fiction
Non Fiction and Westerns

Special interest titles available in large print are:
The Little Oxford Dictionary
Music Book, Song Book
Hymn Book, Service Book

Also available from us courtesy of Oxford University Press:
Young Readers' Dictionary
(large print edition)
Young Readers' Thesaurus
(large print edition)

For further information or a free brochure, please contact us at:
Ulverscroft Large Print Books Ltd.,
The Green, Bradgate Road, Anstey,
Leicester, LE7 7FU, England.
Tel: (00 44) **0116 236 4325**
Fax: (00 44) **0116 234 0205**

Other titles in the
Linford Romance Library:

THE LOCKET OF LOGAN HALL

Christina Garbutt

Newly widowed Emily believes she will never love again. Working as an assistant in flirtatious Cameron's antiques shop, she finds a romantic keepsake in an old writing desk. Emily and Cameron set off on a hunt for the original owner, and the discoveries they make on the way change both of them forever. But Emily doesn't realise that Cameron is slowly falling in love with her. Is his love doomed to be unrequited, or will Emily see what's right in front of her — before it's too late?

PARADISE FOUND

Sarah Purdue

Carrie's first visit to Chatterham House, where her grandparents lived and worked, becomes an unexpected turning point in her life when her relationship with her boyfriend ends disastrously there; but she meets Edward, a handsome employee who shares her interest in the estate's history. When she begins volunteering at the house on weekends, she feels drawn to Edward — but the icily beautiful Portia seems to have a claim on him, and his only explanation is that it's 'complicated'. Will Carrie decide he's worth risking her heart for?

A MERRY BRAMBLEWICK CHRISTMAS

Sharon Booth

Recovering from a break-up, Izzy is throwing herself into the primary school Christmas play — it's a huge project, even with fellow teacher and volunteer assistant Ash by her side. As Christmas draws nearer and the snow begins to fall, Izzy and Ash develop a warm and growing attraction. But Izzy's best friend Anna has been acting coldly towards her since she revealed the reason her last relationship ended. With Anna judging her so harshly, dare Izzy tell Ash the truth about herself and risk everything they have built so far?

KINDRED HEARTS

Wendy Kremer

After a humiliating break-up, Kate decides to spend Christmas alone in a secluded countryside cottage. But her plans for solitude evaporate when she meets the guest at the neighbouring cottage — exciting, unpredictable Alex. As Kate continues to bump into Alex in unexpected places, her oldest and best friend Chris warns her off her new acquaintance. She is furious — who is he to interfere? But as she realises that Alex might not be what she is searching for, Kate wonders if she's been looking for love in all the wrong places . . .